The Silent Dead
A Solomon Gray Novel

The Silent Dead
Published by Gladius Press 2019
Copyright © Keith Nixon 2019
First Edition
Keith Nixon has asserted his right under the Copyright, Designs and Patents Act 1998 to be identified as the author of this work.
CONDITIONS OF SALE
All rights reserved. No part of this publication may be reproduced, stored in a retrieval system, or transmitted in any form or by any means, electronic, mechanical, photocopying, scanning, recording or otherwise, without the prior permission of the publisher.
This book has been sold subject to the condition that it shall not, by way of trade or otherwise, be lent, resold, hired out, or otherwise circulated without the publisher's prior consent in any form of binding or cover other than that in which it is published and without a similar condition including this condition being imposed on the subsequent purchaser.
All characters in this publication are fictitious and any resemblance to real persons, living or dead is purely coincidental.
Cover design by James Webber.

One

Detective Inspector Solomon Gray drove past three patrol cars bumped up onto the kerb outside the address he wanted. There wasn't anywhere else to pull in. Most of the properties on Ranelagh Grove, a quiet back street in St. Peter's, were built long before vehicles and parking were a necessity. He circled around again, circumnavigating the Elim Oasis Pentecostal church in the centre; a bland, single storey brick structure with a pitch roof surrounded by a moat of grass.

He finally drew up in the only available space – across a neighbour's driveway and next to a small knot of bystanders standing on the corner, trying to work out what was going on. Residents in this quiet corner of Thanet were unused to a police investigation which erupted without warning earlier that morning.

Gray got out of his car, ignored the tut from one of the group, seemingly irritated by where he'd chosen to park. Gray made for the house, a double fronted brick and flint property. The uniformed police constable on duty by the front door threw a sloppy salute as Gray entered the narrow front garden through a white wooden fence. "A bit parky, Sol," said PC Damian Boughton.

Although it was January, Boughton, his usual beat central Margate, wore only a thin black standard issue jacket more suited to the summer. Gray was wrapped up tight in a padded coat, the cold already seeping through. Boughton proved a stocky, imposing figure. Useful in Margate where, compared to St. Peter's, trouble came as standard.

But Gray's mind lay more on what was inside, rather than the weather. "Where is it?"

Boughton pointed to the window above their heads, said, "First floor." He shivered as he said, "It's ghoulish."

"You've seen it?"

"Course. You'd have to, right? My old dad told me he'd come across these things more than once, and his dad did too, regularly. Not so common these days." Boughton moved out of Gray's way. "That's progress for you."

"One word for it."

"Good luck."

Gray entered the house, finding himself in a narrow, unlit and silent hallway. Bare wooden floorboards and stairs of stripped wood in front, a door to a living room on one side, a multitude of pictures on the cream painted wall opposite. He glanced at the nearest frame. Photos of people in small groups, adults and children. All seemingly, different.

He headed up the stairs, reached a landing. The door to every room stood open on its hinges. Detective Constable Melanie Pfeffer, petite and blonde, waited for him in the entrance furthest away. "Sir, in here."

She'd cut her hair recently so it was very short, a flick across her forehead, shaved tight at the sides, and sported another black eye which they would need to again discuss – if that was the word for it.

But not now.

He passed into what was clearly the master bedroom, given the space and perspective. Two sash windows, the curtains, drawn wide, looked out onto the church below. A double bed made up and neat, the brass bedstead gleaming, to the right, a large gilt-edged mirror on the wall above. The light brown carpet deep and thick. Opposite, a wide wardrobe in a dark, polished wood. It stood empty, the clothes which had been inside draped over a chair, coat hangers still hooked into the necks of blouses and dresses.

Detective Sergeant Ted Ibbotson was waiting between the bed and window, a tall man who regularly wore trousers that were too short for him, revealing trademark white socks at the ankle, and large feet. Ibbotson's hands were clasped in front of him, head bowed, as if he were in church himself, and showing a monk's patch of balding pate. He was in his early 40s, recently back at work after an extended sick period. Pfeffer hung behind, at Gray's shoulder.

On the duvet was a cardboard box, longer than it was wide, the flaps open. The supplier's brand and an adhesive address label were obvious on the outside.

"Is this it?" asked Gray.

"Yes, sir," Ibbotson said in a hushed tone. He shook his head. A positive and a negative. "They thought it was a doll at first."

"They?"

"The son and daughter of the recently deceased homeowner."

Gray took a pace closer, leaned over and peered inside. He'd been warned about the contents, but still the breath caught in his throat. All his years in CID and this was truly a first.

The 'it' they'd all been referring to did seem to be a child's toy. Only the face visible, the body wrapped head to foot in a blanket. Eyes closed – they would be blue, of course – skin the colour and appearance of old parchment paper. Pale puckered lips and a tuft of dark hair poking out from beneath the cloth.

A baby.

Mummified.

Stored in a box hidden in the back of a wardrobe for who knew how long or why.

"Oh my God," said Gray.

Two

T he baby appeared just weeks, maybe even only days old. But that was just an educated guess. Although Gray had had children it had been years ago.

Gray checked the address on the label. This house. He retreated, said, "Take me back to the beginning."

Ibbotson carefully closed the flaps, hiding the body from view before he spoke. "The homeowner was one Andrea Ogilvy." Same as on the label. "She died eleven days ago and was buried in St. Peter's." Ibbotson pointed in broadly the right direction. He meant the Anglican Church a couple of streets away, not the Elim across the road. Nobody got buried there. Gray knew St. Peter's very well. He'd married, baptised his children and buried his ex-wife there. He used to worship too.

Not anymore.

Ibbotson continued, "Her kids, Polly and Philip, were in the process of clearing out the house and came across this." Ibbotson meant the baby. "They called us straightaway." Ibbotson shook his head.

"Where are they now?"

"In the kitchen, sir. Got them a sweet tea each and some company. Dr Clough is on his way." Thanet's forensic pathologist. "He should be here soon."

"Good, thank you."

"It's what I'm here for, sir." Gray managed not to roll his eyes. They moved onto the landing. "I assume you want to talk to the pair of them?"

"I'd just like a quick word with DC Pfeffer first."

Ibbotson's gaze flicked between Gray and Pfeffer. "Okay."

Gray pointed to the room next door, a dusty space filled with boxes. He entered, Pfeffer following. Gray pulled the door to, the click of the latch loud.

"Have you been fighting again?" asked Gray.

"Should we be doing this now?"

"Yes."

Pfeffer huffed. "We've been over this, Sol. It's called boxing. And you know why I do it."

A few months ago, Pfeffer had been badly beaten and hospitalised. She'd changed – more introverted, not so quick to laugh.

"And I'll say again, it doesn't look great for one of my officers to turn up to work bruised."

"That's what I am now, one of your officers?"

"Strictly, nothing's different."

"Sleeping together doesn't count?"

"Keep your voice down!" Gray couldn't help but snap. Ibbotson would more than likely have his ear to the door. "That's over."

"Now your girlfriend's back." She meant Emily Wyatt, who'd recently been stationed in Margate after the conclusion of an operation she'd been working on in another county.

"It's difficult."

"No, it really isn't."

"Now's not the right time to discuss us."

"Neither was the last three occasions I brought this particular subject up. And you started the conversation this time."

"I meant about the boxing."

"So, you get to pick and choose the subject?" Pfeffer crossed her arms. "Anyway, I've quit the training for now. There will be no more bruises."

"Glad I finally got through to you."

Pfeffer opened her mouth to respond but was interrupted by a knock at the door. Ibbotson stuck his head round. "Apologies, Dr Clough is here."

"One moment," said Gray. He turned back to Pfeffer. "You were saying?"

Pfeffer shook her head. "You're right. Let's do this later." She moved past Gray, swung the door wide revealing Dr Ben Clough, holding a black leather medical bag. He nodded, seemingly oblivious to the atmosphere between Gray and Pfeffer. Clough was wiry, bespectacled.

"Where am I needed?" asked Clough.

"I'll show you," said Pfeffer.

Once Clough and Pfeffer were gone Ibbotson, leaning against the bannister, asked, "Everything all right, sir? With Pfeffer, I mean."

"We're fine."

"If I can do anything to help, as your sergeant, I mean, I'm here for you."

"I appreciate it." Gray didn't. "For now, just show me to the kitchen, please."

"Sure." Ibbotson led Gray down the stairs.

Gray regarded the framed photos as he followed, hand on the bannister. All the images contained children of various ages. Dozens of them. Most smiling, some not.

"Andrea Ogilvy, she was a foster carer," said Ibbotson by way of explanation. He'd paused on the bottom step, watching Gray. "Bet it used to be a noisy place. Quiet as the grave, now." Ibbotson turned and continued to a door at the end of the corridor, held it open to allow Gray to pass through first into a brightly lit space. There were kitchen units to one side, then, beyond, a conservatory which opened onto the garden. To the right a sizeable, round table. More photos on the wall overlooking the occupants.

Three people turned towards Gray. All seated, each with a mug in front of them. It didn't seem like he'd interrupted a conversation. A man and a woman Gray didn't recognise and one he did. The latter being Detective Constable Jerry Worthington, Newcastle born and bred, a broad-shouldered man from spending time in the gym and playing rugby. Gray glanced at Ibbotson, who was inscrutable. Worthington was supposed to be staying in the station, not out on investigations.

Bloody Ibbotson.

"Cuppa, sir?" asked Worthington, he half rose, ready to serve.

"No," said Gray. He wouldn't drink anything offered by him.

Worthington sat back down. "This is Polly Draper and her brother, Philip Ogilvy."

Ogilvy was grey haired, deep frown lines on his forehead, crooked square teeth. His hands were clasped around the mug, the skin worn, nails bitten down. He looked like a labourer or a gardener. His sister was younger with dark hair, high cheekbones and pale skin.

"If you wouldn't mind, DC Worthington, I'd like to speak with Miss Draper and Mr Ogilvy alone."

Worthington flicked a glance over Gray's shoulder at Ibbotson.

"Is that all, sir?" asked the sergeant.

"We'll talk later," said Gray.

Worthington stood. Something growled as he did so. A small-ish dog, white with black and brown patches, half in, half out of a basket on the floor, teeth bared. Gray didn't recognise the breed, he knew little about dogs. There hadn't been the time for a pet when he'd had a family and no inclination since. Particularly since he'd moved into a flat which didn't possess a garden.

"That's Mack," said Draper.

"He's a bloody mutt," said Ogilvy, his tone a growl too.

Worthington shifted and a warning rumbled in Mack's throat again. Gray decided he liked the dog. Anyone who wasn't keen on Worthington was fine with him.

"It's okay to stroke him," said Draper. "He's normally very placid."

Gray went over, squatted down and stroked Mack. The dog sat, Gray saw his own reflection in the dog's large brown doleful eyes. The dog flopped down, rolled over onto his back, paws raised. Gray rubbed the dog's chest. He could feel ribs under the skin.

"That's amazing," said Draper. She stood by his shoulder. "He's been totally lost since Mum died. In fact, this is the first time he's moved from his basket. He's barely eaten anything, and we've had to carry him outside. He does his business then it's straight back to his bed. Isn't that right, Philip?"

"Don't bring me into this," said Ogilvy. "I want nothing more to do with the animal. And picking up his crap." Ogilvy shuddered. "No chance."

"Thanks for reminding me, Philip," said Draper.

Gray stood upright, went back to the table, pulled out a chair. Just the three of them now, excluding Mack.

"I'm Detective Inspector Solomon Gray."

"Polly, Philip," said Draper. "And I'm Mrs, not Miss as your officer stated."

"My apologies."

"Not your fault."

"I understand your mother died recently, I'm sorry for your loss."

"Thank you."

Gray felt a nudge at his leg. He glanced down. It was Mack. Another nudge of Gray's calf with his nose.

"If he annoys you, just kick him away," said Ogilvy.

"Philip!" Draper frowned at her brother.

"What?" Ogilvy raised his arms, attempting innocence.

"He's okay." Gray reached down and stroked the dog around his ears. Mack licked his hand. Gray wiped his palm on his trouser leg, hoping Draper didn't see. Mack nudged him again before sighing and lying down, chin resting on Gray's foot.

"He's as tired as we are," said Draper. "I've been coming here every day to feed him." Ogilvy frowned, turned his head away.

"I understand you discovered the baby while you were sorting through your mother's things?" asked Gray.

"Philip found her, didn't you?" Ogilvy shook his head, like he didn't want to be part of that conversation either.

"How do you know it's a her?" There wasn't any way to tell so far as Gray had seen.

"I don't but calling a child 'it' feels wrong." Exactly what Gray had done. "Philip was taking clothes out of the wardrobe. I was in the next bedroom, heard a shriek and came running. Philip just stood there, pale, holding the box out towards me. It was mind-numbing, frankly. We stared at her for a while, then called the police."

"I didn't shriek." Ogilvy glared at his sister.

"Do you have any idea why she might have been there?" asked Gray.

"None." Ogilvy was sharp. "I've never felt the need to search my parent's wardrobe until now. Why would I? And they never mentioned anything about a baby's corpse being under our roof."

"Can you tell me about them? Your parents?"

"Our father passed eight years ago," said Draper. "He was a manager at a local chemicals plant. Retired at 65, was gone within a year. Mum was a little older than him, 78 when she died."

"I understand your mother was a foster carer?"

"She looked after hundreds of children over the years. It was her mission, so to speak. After Philip she thought she couldn't get pregnant again, so other people's kids became hers, then one day..." Draper glanced at her brother. "I unexpectedly came along." Draper pointed at the photos on the wall beside them. "These are just a few of the many she looked after."

"Kept life interesting, I expect?"

"Mum didn't make it easy on herself or us. She often took the challenging ones. That had run away from home, possessed learning difficulties, unplanned for pregnancies. It was bedlam sometimes. Council staff turning up at all times of the day and night. Sometimes the kids would be here for only a few hours, others for months."

"It was awful," said Ogilvy with a scowl. "You never knew who was going to be in your house, even in your bed. One of them crapped in my sock drawer once." He shuddered.

"Don't listen to him," said Draper. "It was a constant adventure. Mum, she simply cared about others. She couldn't help herself."

"What about babies? Would they be brought round?" It was the obvious question for Gray to ask.

"Not often but sometimes, sure."

"When did your mother stop fostering?"

"Just after she turned 70."

"Why?"

"It wasn't lack of energy; I can tell you." Draper laughed. "She had enough drive for all three of us."

"So, what was the reason?"

"Because the council were bastards," cut in Ogilvy, banging his fist on the table.

"You know it wasn't just that, Philip," said Draper.

"They treated her very badly."

"What do you mean?" asked Gray.

"There was a complaint." Ogilvy stared at the mug he was turning between his fingers. "One of the girls said our dad was spying on her, touching her up."

"Utter bullshit," snapped Ogilvy.

"Nothing like it had ever happened before. Until then our parents had faultless records. But the council had new rules, the victim was always believed first and foremost."

"Victim, my backside," Ogilvy cut in.

Draper ignored her brother and continued, "Their licence to foster was suspended while the council investigated. It took months, even though the process was supposed to be informal. Nothing was found, of course, and it transpired this girl had lied before. The licence was reinstated, but the experience of the council investigation drained my mother of the desire to put herself out for others anymore."

"It was their lack of belief that hurt them the most." Bitterness in Ogilvy's tone. "People they'd worked with for years and knew them very well just assumed he was guilty."

"It was the process, Philip. They didn't have any choice."

"That's not true, and you know it. What about the presumption of innocence until proven otherwise?"

Gray cut in. "Then what happened?"

"She didn't foster again," said Draper. "The joy was gone out of it. A few months later father died, and mum carried on living here all by herself. That's what wore her down in the end, I think. Being in a silent house full of memories." Draper glanced at the photos on the wall.

Ogilvy turned towards Draper, Gray momentarily forgotten. "But she wasn't alone." He meant the baby.

"What if it was hers?"

"Don't."

"A brother or sister."

"God, no. I can't believe that."

"There is a way of finding out," said Gray.

"What?" asked Ogilvy.

"A DNA test."

"How do they work?" asked Draper.

"If you consent then one of my team will take a swab from the inside of your mouth. We'll also obtain a sample from the baby and compare the results."

"And from that you'll be able to tell?"

"The tests are accurate these days, as much as 99% if there's a match."

Draper glanced at Ogilvy then back to Gray. "I'm okay with that," she said.

"Mr Ogilvy?" asked Gray.

"Would my DNA be stored on a government computer somewhere?"

"It's called the National DNA Database, Mr Ogilvy. And the information will be used purely for comparative purposes. Afterwards your DNA will be destroyed. Only profiles from guilty people are retained." Anyone arrested for an offence had to give a DNA sample. It was a powerful tool Gray believed in.

"What about the record?"

"Deleted too. Because of the new data protection act."

"I'm still not convinced."

"Surely we need to know?" said Draper.

"Is there any other way, Inspector?" asked Ogilvy.

"There may be other information, like on the birth register. However, if the birth wasn't documented then in all likelihood we'd never get a complete answer for you."

"Philip, please," said Draper.

Eventually Ogilvy nodded. "All right, just for you, sis."

Three

Gray bent down, stroked Mack again. "Come on little fella, I've got to get on." The dog raised his chin from Gray's foot.

"Could I ask you a favour?" said Draper.

"I've things to do."

"It's nothing too onerous and won't take much time. Would you mind seeing if you could get Mack to eat something?"

"I'm hardly a dog whisperer, Mrs Draper."

"As I said earlier, he's not responded to anyone else until now. Please, it may really help."

"All right. First just let me get the DNA samples organised."

"Great." Draper smiled. "Thanks."

Clough was walking down the stairs as Gray left the kitchen. Mack followed close behind and got in the way as Gray attempted to shut the door.

"Mack, here," called Draper, but the dog didn't move, staring up at Gray with his dark, unblinking eyes. Draper came over, took Mack by the collar and pulled him back. "Sorry about that." Gray closed the door and the dog whined.

Clough, holding his black leather medical bag, was waiting for him. "Looks like you've got a new friend."

"Our relationship will be brief, at best," said Gray. Clough laughed. "Any initial opinions on the baby?"

"They're just assessments, of course. I can't be definitive yet."

"I understand."

"There's no external signs as to cause of death that I can see, although there could be some on the torso, of course. We'll need a post-mortem to determine a potential root cause. Mummification is a process of heat and time. Recently born babies have very little in the way of bacteria in their bodies so, the normal stages of the body breaking down don't occur. Based on her size, I would estimate that she was only days old when she died. However, the mummification makes that an approximation. And as for when she died, it's impossible to say at this stage."

"When will you schedule the PM?"

"Tomorrow, more than likely. Mummification isn't something I've come across before. I need to do some reading up on it."

"I'll make sure I'm there."

"I've arranged for an ambulance to collect the body. It should arrive any time."

"Bloody sad."

"Parents should never outlive their kids."

"Who says she did?"

"True."

"Otherwise I'll be in touch about the procedure." Clough shook hands. They were cold and dry. As always. "See you soon."

"Unfortunately."

Clough let himself out of the front door.

What sounded like a creaking floorboard came from the stairs. Pfeffer was on the landing. "I overheard what the doctor said."

"It wasn't confidential."

"I know, I just didn't want to interrupt." She came down halfway. "All these children."

"Takes a special kind of commitment to look after other people's kids. Your own are hard enough."

Pfeffer stared at Gray, made as if to say something.

The front door opened. Boughton, constable's custodian helmet in hand, said, "Ambulance is here, sir. For the body."

"I'll show them up," said Pfeffer.

"No, I need you to take DNA swabs for Draper and Ogilvy," said Gray.

"Let me handle the boys in green," offered Boughton. Gray raised a thumb.

"The DNA kit is in the car," said Pfeffer. She retreated out of sight as the paramedics entered and went up the stairs, preceded by Boughton, leaving Gray wondering what she might have been about to say and without a chance to ask.

Draper was at the kitchen door, holding onto Mack's collar. "Are you free now?"

"Briefly." Gray had hoped he could make his escape, but it wasn't to be.

On the kitchen unit was an empty ceramic bowl, a large bag of dry food and a tin of meat. Draper had even popped the can lid for him. She handed him a fork.

"You want me to prepare it for him?"

"It's not Michelin stuff," said Ogilvy.

"Shut up, Philip," said Draper. "It's best if he sees you getting everything ready. I'd suggest a handful of the dry food first."

Gray was reaching an arm into the bag when Pfeffer entered. She paused, staring at him. "Do you want me to come back later?"

"Who are you?" asked Ogilvy, the attitude gone from his tone, a half smile on his lips.

"DC Pfeffer. She's here to take the DNA samples," said Gray.

"I'm sure the lady could have answered for herself, isn't that right?"

Pfeffer put the box she was carrying on the table, extracted a vial, said to Ogilvy, "Can you open your mouth, please?"

"Happily." Ogilvy showed his teeth, then cracked his jaw. Pfeffer leant in, rubbed a swab around inside Ogilvy's mouth before placing it into the vial and screwing the cap on. She labelled the bottle and slid it into a bag.

Pfeffer turned to Draper. "Your turn, ma'am."

"Just put half the can of meat on top of the biscuits and place it down over there for Mack." Draper pointed at a white plastic mat in the conservatory. There was a black and white print of a dog on it.

Gray did as he was told while Pfeffer dealt with Draper. By the time the bowl was down Pfeffer was done. "Thanks," she said and left.

"This is great." Draper nodded towards Mack, who was greedily chomping down the food.

"Who cares?" said Ogilvy. "What's next with the tests?"

"They'll be sent to an accredited laboratory for analysis. Feedback will be in a few days, a week at most."

"Can it be her that gives me the results?" Ogilvy meant Pfeffer.

"It'll be me." Gray handed Draper a business card and left another on the unit for Ogilvy.

"Shame, I was hoping one decent thing might have come from today."

"I'll be in touch."

Gray left the kitchen and glanced inside the front room. The space was dominated by a bay window. Nets hung across the glass; thick red curtains held by tie backs. The furniture was all dark wood and heavy. A sofa, squashy chairs, a table beneath the window. A mantlepiece over an open fireplace was littered with framed photographs. He looked at them briefly, more faces he didn't know.

Outside, Boughton was back on the doorstep, Pfeffer a few yards away, leaning into the rear of her car.

"All sorted with the paramedics?" asked Gray.

"They're gone. And so is the shoebox baby," said Boughton.

"The what?"

"Worthington came up with it. Snappy, right?"

"Not really."

"By the way, Sol. Would you be free for a beer one evening after work? There's something I'd like to talk to you about."

"What?"

Pfeffer straightened up, shut the car door, went to the front.

"Not here, though," said Boughton.

She opened the door, got inside.

"Excuse me, I just want to have a word with Melanie."

Boughton grabbed hold of Gray's arm, pulled him back. "It's important, Sol."

"I'll call you when I'm free."

"Promise?"

"Of course." By the time Gray got loose from Boughton's grip Pfeffer was pulling away. If she saw him waving at her in the rear-view mirror, she made no sign of it.

Gray passed by Boughton on the way to his own car. He heard a bark. There, in the window, was Mack, front feet planted on the sill, watching Gray.

"Looks like you've got a new friend," said Boughton.

Gray snorted. "That's what Clough said."

"You know, it's weird. Only moments ago, Pfeffer was saying she was surprised you even had the compassion to look after a dog, never mind a child."

"A child?"

"That's what I thought. The baby's dead, right?" Boughton pulled a face, like Pfeffer was crazy. "Anyway, I'll call you later."

THE FLINT–BUILT CHURCH loomed over its immediate surroundings. A crenelated tower, more castle than place of worship, pushed up towards the sky. Beneath stood the vicarage and burial ground. Across the road was a supermarket and car park where Gray had left his vehicle next to some large community recycling bins.

He entered the grounds through a side gate. It had been a couple of years since he was last here, but there wasn't much change. Trees and bushes grew between the stones and statues to the forgotten dead. A war grave kept pristine, an angel minus arms and just the one wing.

The most recent internments, in a rectangle of open space, were the furthest from the church. He followed a narrow tarmac path, as straight as any Roman road, away from the church. At the far end was a relatively new area added a couple of decades ago, giving more room for burials, although it soon filled and space in the graveyard remained a premium. The markers here were more ordered, arranged in regimented lines, and tightly packed. Beyond, the path continued through cabbage fields and then passed the Queen Elizabeth the Queen Mother hospital before entering the edge of Margate.

Andrea Ogilvy's plot was in the corner. The stone was polished marble, the gold inscription bright and unfaded. Her name looked to have been carved into the existing marble and the original lettering refreshed – she'd been buried with her husband. The earth was freshly dug. Too early in the year to put grass down, like over all the others. Some flowers stood in a pot; the blooms shriveled by the overnight frost. Gray pondered over the grave for a moment.

But really, he wasn't here for Andrea.

So, he retraced his steps. To nearby, where his ex-wife, Kate, had been laid to rest, about the time Andrea Ogilvy had stopped fostering. Weeds, their leaves brown and withered, had grown up and over the inscription since he'd last visited. Kate's family was all gone now, meaning there was nobody beside him to care for the space. Feeling twinges of guilt; he bent down and pulled away the encroaching greenery, yanked the plants out by the roots and tossed them into an overgrown area to one side.

Next to Kate's grave was an empty space. She'd obtained it for their missing son, Tom, shortly before her own death, but it remained untouched. Gray's eyes couldn't long linger before he moved to the adjacent stone. That space was overgrown too, the inscription on the cheap headstone faded and hard to read. Zara Jessop died from an unspecified reason at 18.

Life could be cruel sometimes.

Four

Gray entered Odell House, the police station on Fort Hill, in Margate. The design was classic unimaginative 1970s – a plain brick box, white plastic windows and a flat roof which occasionally leaked. However, the view over the English Channel made up for lazy architecture. And there was a pub, The Britannia, right next door.

The CID team was located in the Detectives' Office, a collection of desks grouped together in clusters, each with a phone, computer and screen. In one corner stood a makeshift kitchen, in the other Gray's own small office. Gray hung up his coat.

Worthington, the irritant himself, was at his desk, the space opposite his, where Ibbotson usually sat, empty. A large spider plant occupied one corner of Ibbotson's desk, spilling over the edge. Ibbotson was an itch Gray wanted to scratch but that would have to wait for now, it seemed. He paused between Pfeffer and Wyatt who were seated at their respective desks either side of the passageway.

"Can I get either of you a drink?" asked Gray.

Wyatt tapped her mug, said, "I'm good, thanks." She'd recently relocated to Margate when her previous assignment, Operation Pivot, an initiative to tackle County Lines drug supply, had concluded. She lived nearby in Deal, a forty-minute drive away. Prior to Pivot she'd worked for The

Child Exploitation and Online Protection Command, CEOP, part of the National Crime Agency.

Gray's boss, Detective Chief Inspector Yvonne Hamson, had agreed Wyatt could base herself in Margate until she was reassigned, which had created some interesting stresses. Thankfully Wyatt and Hamson oblivious to them.

"Melanie?"

Pfeffer didn't as much as glance at Gray. "I'm good." She being the primary source of the tension.

"Either of you seen Ibbotson anywhere?"

"Sorry, not since you came back from St. Peter's," said Wyatt. "Why?"

"Private matter."

Wyatt winked at Pfeffer, but she was paying the other woman no attention. Gray went to the kitchen area, added just enough water to the kettle.

Wyatt joined him as he flicked it on. "Actually, I will have a freshen up." She poured what was left of her drink into the sink, washed it out then picked up the kettle, sloshed the contents around, added more water from the tap.

Pfeffer glanced over her shoulder, frowned briefly before returning her attention to her PC screen. Gray wasn't sure if the glare was at him, Wyatt or both of them.

He and Pfeffer had had a brief, no-strings-attached fling. At the same time Gray was in a long-distance relationship with Wyatt. Gray had broken it off with Pfeffer when Wyatt announced she was to be stationed in Margate. Unsurprisingly, Pfeffer was cool with both Wyatt and Gray. He constantly expected to be found out, for the past to come back and savage him. Sometimes he even wondered if that's what Pfeffer wanted.

"You should boil a full one," said Wyatt.

"Why? Most of it goes cold. Does my head in. Such a waste." Stuff like this wouldn't have bothered him a few years ago.

"You're turning into a moaning old git."

"Maybe."

"I heard about the baby in the box, the poor mite," said Wyatt, leaning against the counter, right beside Gray. "It's the talk of the station."

"I'm not surprised."

"The shoebox baby I heard it called."

"Worthington?"

"He's very pleased with himself. It makes you think, though."

"What does?"

"You know." Wyatt leaned in. "Children."

"Is there enough for me?" asked Pfeffer loudly, although she was only a few feet away.

"Plenty," said Wyatt. She smiled at Pfeffer but got just teeth in return, no genuine emotion behind it.

"Considerate of you to look out for both of us, sir." Pfeffer leaned in. Wyatt reluctantly took a pace sideways, giving Pfeffer room to grab the kettle. Wyatt raised her eyebrows at Gray as Pfeffer splashed water onto a tea bag.

"You might know this, Emily," asked Gray. "Who would I speak to at social services regarding foster care?"

"Why, are you thinking of getting a kid?"

"God, no! I'm long done with that kind of thing."

Pfeffer knocked her cup over, spilling hot water everywhere. "Bloody hell!"

Wyatt grabbed a roll of paper towel, tore off several strips, passed them to Pfeffer and started to mop up the mess.

"I'm fine," said Pfeffer.

"You okay?" Wyatt asked Pfeffer.

"I said, I'm fine!"

"All right." Wyatt reached for the tea bags to make Pfeffer another drink.

"I can do that too."

Wyatt raised her hands in surrender at Gray as Pfeffer finished cleaning.

"I'll come back when you're done," said Pfeffer and retreated.

"What was that all about?" asked Wyatt.

"I've no idea," lied Gray. "Hormones?"

"Brilliant." Wyatt's expression was flat and unimpressed. "Hormones explain everything about a woman, right?"

"Anyway, back to social services. I'd like to speak with someone about the process of fostering because the person whose house we found the baby in was a carer."

"The shoebox baby."

"I'm not using that phrase."

"The baby in the box is quite a mouthful."

"Will you check, or not?"

"Of course."

"Thanks."

Wyatt glanced around the office area before sliding closer. "What about going out for dinner soon? I feel like I've hardly seen you."

"Sure, I'd like that."

"Good." She squeezed his arm. "See you later."

"Don't forget to make that call."

"It's only been a minute; I haven't got dementia." Wyatt rolled her eyes and walked away.

Gray returned to his office, wiggled his mouse and woke up his laptop. There was an email waiting him from Clough confirming the PM on the baby for first thing tomorrow morning.

Gray entered the Police National Computer database and searched for Andrea Ogilvy. Three records were returned. Two noise complaints from neighbours; some shouting and screaming late at night a few months apart. Uniform had attended and spoken with both parties.

The third was from a family on behalf of whom Andrea had temporarily housed a child. The allegation was that Andrea's husband, Gordon, had been spying on one of the children. However, the follow-up notes stated the claim was unsubstantiated and taken no further.

"Here you go." It was Wyatt in the entrance, holding out a yellow post-it note. "Alexander Vardie, he's a senior practitioner. The frontline social services team report into him."

"That was quick." Gray took the note.

"I don't hang around, Sol. You should know that." Wyatt winked and left.

Gray picked up his phone, dialed Vardie's number, but the call simply rang before dropping into voicemail. "Mr Vardie, this is DI Gray from Thanet Police. I'd appreciate it if you could call me back on this number. There's an important matter I'd like to discuss with you."

Just then Ibbotson wandered into the Detectives' Office, wiping his hands on his trousers, meaning he'd just come from the toilets. As Ibbotson passed by Worthington he patted him on the shoulder.

Gray stood and called to Ibbotson from his doorway. "Ted. I'd like a word." Worthington looked over his shoulder, but Gray ignored him.

"Of course, sir." Ibbotson was usually a pleaser. Ibbotson never said no to any request from a senior officer. Gray suspected that if he asked Ibbotson to jump out of a window the man probably would. Yet he'd ignored a direct request from Gray regarding Worthington which made it all the more surprising.

"In my office."

The sergeant blinked. When the sergeant was inside the room Gray closed the door then leant against it, arms crossed.

"What's the matter, sir? I hope I haven't done something wrong?"

"Why was DC Worthington in St Peter's today?"

"Sir?"

"It's a simple question. DC Worthington is not supposed to work outside of the station unless expressly agreed by me."

"I thought it would be a good idea to bring him back into the fold, as it were."

"Do you recall our first discussion after your return to work interview?"

"DC Worthington."

"And my view of how I wanted you to manage him and his behavior going forward, right?"

"I remember."

"And in turn I clearly recall you stating you understood and would act accordingly, right?" Ibbotson nodded. "Then what the bloody hell happened to the 'not unless expressly agreed with me', part sergeant?"

"Nothing."

"Meaning you deliberately ignored my request?"

"Not exactly, sir. You see, I've been spending quite a bit of time with Jerry and in my opinion he's a really decent bloke. He's capable and we're short-handed. It seemed wrong not to use him properly."

"By wrong, you mean I'm wrong?"

"I didn't say that, sir."

"Not in so many words. You didn't discuss any of this with me first. Why?"

"Sir, as your sergeant I do have the opportunity to use my initiative from time to time. You're extremely busy."

"And as your inspector I'm able to hand down my wishes and expect them to be adhered to. In this case you expressly went against my order." Ibbotson cast his eyes down, shifted from foot to foot. "What's on your mind?"

"It's just..." Ibbotson shook his head. "I probably shouldn't say, sir."

"Go on, I'm giving you permission – this time."

"Okay, it's just people think you're biased against Jerry." Ibbotson stared straight at Gray now. Ibbotson was correct; Gray did have a prejudice, and with good reason. "That you don't like him." Also, true. "And your perspective isn't right."

Here, Ibbotson was mistaken. Worthington was a dirty cop, only Gray couldn't prove it. Not yet. So, Gray had been making Worthington's life as difficult as possible until the evidence came to light. Except, Ibbotson seemingly wanted to act as a buffer between them.

"Who are these *people*, sergeant?"

Ibbotson took on a pained expression. "I'd rather not say. I was told in confidence."

"Would 'they' happen to be one Jerry Worthington?"

Ibbotson straightened up, like Gray was insulting him and Ibbotson took exception. "Not at all!"

"Really?"

"Sir, I'm not a liar!"

"Let me make this very plain, sergeant. I *do* have a problem with Worthington and it's not something I'm going to spend time explaining to you now or in the future other than saying my reasons are valid and supported by DCI Hamson. Worthington is well aware of my feelings too. I expect him here in the station from now on until I say otherwise. I don't want any further lateral thinking by you or anybody else on this matter and I do not want you listening to anything Worthington has to tell you. Is that plain enough for you and these people?"

"One hundred per cent, sir. Is that all?"

"Yes." As Ibbotson's hand was reaching for the door handle Gray said, "Ted."

Ibbotson glanced over his shoulder. "Sir?"

"Be careful of Worthington. He's not who or what you think he is."

"Door open or closed, sir?"

"Open, thanks."

Gray watched Ibbotson stalk back across the office and drop into his chair. Worthington must have said something because Ibbotson's eyes flicked up to Gray before he shook his head at his younger colleague.

Gray suspected Ibbotson would continue his one-man crusade on Worthington's behalf. If he did then he'd find himself sharing a sinking boat with his desk mate.

"Are you all right?" Pfeffer, in the doorway.

"It's nothing."

"Don't be fooled by Ibbotson," she said. "He's passive aggressive, that one."

"I've worked with his type before. What can I do for you?"

"Just to let you know I've organised a courier to get the DNA samples into the FSP for analysis."

The Forensic Service Provider was a Government approved accredited laboratory; private companies operating under contract to the Home Office and responsible for running the National DNA Database. The NDNAD, as it was otherwise known, had been established in 1995 as a centralised facility for the storage of DNA profiles and was now the largest database of its kind in the world. The service had proven a highly successful tool for solving crimes and now 23 million profiles were stored and continually increasing with every sample of human material, saliva or hair for example, collected from a crime scene being entered. The police were empowered to take DNA samples and retain them if the suspect was convicted of an offence.

FSP technicians evaluated a discrete genome of the otherwise massive DNA chain – just sixteen markers. They also assessed the sex of the person whose DNA they checked. Besides this, the analysis didn't reveal personal aspects like physical appearance or race. There were over 6 million profiles on record, the majority of which were white, northern European and men. NDNAD didn't come without controversy. Civil liberties groups regularly attacked the storage of DNA as a privacy infringement, something Ogilvy had alluded to with his initial protestations about a sample being taken.

"You prioritised it, right?"

"Of course."

"And requested a familial search too?"

Which meant an examination of the DNA database for close relatives, those who shared a significant proportion of their DNA – not an exact match but near enough. Statistically, close relatives lived in or near the immediate proximity of the offender.

"Of course, sir. Some of us don't need to be told what to do all the time."

Gray checked his watch. Kent Police dealt with an FSP up in the Midlands. "The transportation alone will take three or four hours."

"It is what it is and testing probably wouldn't have started until tomorrow morning at the earliest, even if they were right around the corner."

Gray sighed. "I guess."

"What's the rush? This is a cold case."

"People need answers, Melanie."

"People *always* need answers. This one's no different, is it?"

"When children are involved, cases are usually more sensitive, in my experience."

"Can I ask a question?"

"Sure."

Pfeffer stepped further into the office, pushed the door partially closed. "What you said earlier, about being done with kids."

Gray frowned, trying to remember the specifics of the conversation. "Okay."

"Did you mean it?"

"Well, yes. I'm a bit too old for children these days."

Pfeffer was going to say something else but there was a brief rap at the door.

"Sorry to interrupt." Ibbotson, leaning inside, sounding anything but apologetic, a glower still on his face. "We've had a call from the hospital." He checked the notepad in his hand. "A Doctor Maltby. He wanted to let us know about a patient who came into Accident and Emergency at the QEQM earlier, a young man." The QEQM was the Queen Elizabeth the Queen Mother hospital in Margate, not far from the station. "He'd been mauled by a dog. Quite badly."

"I'll leave you to it," said Pfeffer.

"Did you get all you needed?" asked Gray.

"One hundred per cent." Pfeffer retreated.

"Why call us?" asked Gray of Ibbotson.

"Because this wasn't the first time he's seen an attack like this. There's been a couple of dog attacks and on neither occasion has the patient wanted to report it. Doctor Maltby thought we should know. Do you want me to send somebody along?"

"I'll be at the hospital for the PM on the baby tomorrow morning. I'll go to A&E then, see what this is all about."

Gray's internal phone rang. Hamson.

"Have you got five minutes, Sol? I want to discuss the baby in the box."

"Now?"

"Now."

"That's the trouble with superiors," said Ibbotson as Gray put the phone down. "Always unreasonable." He was gone before Gray could respond.

Five

DCI Hamson's office was on the first floor. A large, rain-spattered window in one wall gave a view of the English Channel's choppy brown waters and the traffic travelling along Fort Road. Hamson seated at her desk, her back to the vista, stood as Gray entered, motioned to the conference table tucked in one corner.

"What do we know so far?" asked Hamson.

"Not much. The PM is tomorrow, and DNA tests are scheduled, including a familial search."

"They're bloody expensive," said Hamson.

"The tests themselves aren't."

"Granted, but it could throw up a long list of relatives flung far and wide, each of whom would need tracking down and talking to."

"But what's the other option, we don't check at all? How would that look?"

"Budgets are tight."

"In my humble opinion we should do all we can."

"Humble, you?" Gray shrugged. "You should have checked with me first."

"Why?"

"So, I could talk with Marsh." The Superintendent and a political hack, in Gray's opinion.

Gray made a pfft sound. "Just politics for the sake of it, frankly."

"Managing upwards is essential. You should try it sometimes. If I don't speak with Marsh in advance about stuff like this and it subsequently comes to his attention, then I'm up for a bollocking."

"Getting dizzy up at the top, Von?"

"I'll let you know when I get there. And I've had a visit from Underwood."

Bethany Underwood was the station's press officer. "I didn't realise she was back from maternity."

"For more than a month, Sol."

"We're not really what you'd call friends."

"Is anyone?"

"Do you mean with Underwood or me?"

"Both." Gray frowned. Hamson said, "The press has got wind about the baby in the box."

"Already?"

"A neighbour heard what was going on and called one of the red tops."

"Got to love the salacious press. Anyway," Gray shrugged. "It'll blow over. Something will happen with Brexit to bury the story."

"Actually, it's just the opposite. People are sick of politics and online stories move fast these days. The news has gone viral."

"Sounds like a spreading disease."

"Not far off." Hamson went back to her desk, picked up her laptop, pointed to the screen. "Take a read."

The headline screamed, 'Gruesome Discovery!' above a photo of the house on Ranelagh Grove. Gray frowned as he skimmed. The article described the shock of Ogilvy finding the child as recounted by an unnamed third person – not Ogilvy – followed by several paragraphs of speculation as to who the baby could have been without any actual basis for the assumptions. In a separate text box was a brief biography of Andrea Ogilvy and her time as a foster carer.

"You're the maverick cop, by the way," said Hamson. "Clearly the reporter doesn't know you."

"So I figured." He got through to the end of the article.

"Underwood's phone has been ringing off the hook. She's having a busy time dealing with reporters."

"That's her job, isn't it?"

"Sure, but you know how she is. She'll want to discuss strategy with you."

"Strategy." Gray rolled his eyes. "Jesus."

"Humour her, will you?"

"Is that what we're supposed to do now? Indulge people?" Nobody seemed willing to actually work these days.

"She's just back from having a baby."

"You told me, Von. And I'm not sure why that's relevant. Equal opportunities world and all that."

"Good God, Sol."

He pointed to the laptop screen. "The journalist knows a hell of a lot for an investigation which only started this morning."

"There's a reference to, I quote, a person with intimate knowledge."

"I assumed that was tabloid bullshit."

"Reading the details, I'd tend to think they were telling the truth."

"For once."

"Any thoughts who it could be?"

"One." The obvious choice. "Worthington. He's got form." Worthington had previously been suspected of working with an Albanian gang, providing them with inside information.

"He was there?"

"To my extreme irritation, yes. And it was him who coined the phrase shoebox baby." Hamson screwed up her face in distaste. "Ibbotson decided it would be good for our Geordie friend to get out and about. We've had words."

"Who's running the case?"

"I'm DI, so me."

"Not Ibbotson?"

"He's got enough on his plate."

"Are you sure?"

"Von, we've been through this. I'm not going back to being totally office based. If that's your position I'd rather Ibbotson become DI in my place."

"Which isn't happening."

"Then discussion closed."

Hamson pinched the bridge of her nose. "Whatever. I've got better things to worry about."

"I'm glad we're in agreement."

"Have you got Wyatt involved?"

"I've asked her to contact social services."

"That's it?"

"Why would she do more?"

"Given her previous experience with children it would make sense."

"We don't know enough yet, Von, we've barely scraped the surface."

"How are you two?"

Hamson possessed few friends, yet she and Wyatt had become close, with Gray as their common focus. "We're fine. Really, you don't need to be concerned."

"Okay."

"Why, what's she said?"

"Nothing, just asking."

Gray stared at Hamson for a long moment, but her expression remained unfathomable.

"Anything else I should know?" she asked.

"There's been a dog attack on a kid."

"Oh my God. A child?"

"No, a teenager."

"That doesn't make it any better."

"I wasn't implying it did. We only learned because a concerned medical professional called earlier. The attack sounds deliberate."

"How?"

"The animal was set on the kid, and there's been more than one apparently."

Hamson's phone rang and Gray lost her attention. "Underwood wants to see you as soon as possible."

"I can't right now, I was literally leaving for the hospital when you called," lied Gray.

"Speak with her at your earliest opportunity then, all right?"

"I'll do my best."

Hamson merely raised an eyebrow, picked up the phone. Gray got out while the going was good.

Six

The QEQM, less than a mile and a half and six minutes' drive from the station, took up a large plot of land between two thoroughfares which ran roughly parallel to each other – St. Peter's Road and Ramsgate Road. The rear entrance and maternity wards were off the former, the main entrance and Accident and Emergency off the latter. The original building opened in 1930 then was added to and extended multiple times over the years until it developed into a sprawling site with all manner of facilities of differing vintages organized to make the best of what they had.

Gray pulled into the Ramsgate Road car park then found an empty spot in a small area reserved for the Spencer Private Hospital, a separate wing, where patients coughed up for the privilege (and speed) of treatment but got free parking. He hated paying fees to use a public facility; it was simply wrong.

He walked up the shallow incline towards the entrance. As he got near a taxi pulled up out front and a passenger, a black guy holding a bloody rag to his forehead, exited from the rear.

Large glass doors slid apart. Inside, Gray found himself faced by more doors, which didn't open. He paused. Behind him the taxi passenger sighed, stepped past Gray and nudged a large button off to one side at waist height. Now they opened.

"Go in front of me," said Gray.

"Thanks." Foreign inflection.

Within was the lobby area. It had altered since Gray was last here. Previously it had been decorated in muted colours. Blue, he thought, but wasn't sure. Now it was painted a garish red. To one side remained several rows of seats for waiting patients. Most of the spaces were occupied. The reception area had been screened off by plate glass, reaching up to meet the ceiling, behind which two administrators worked the queue of walking wounded.

Now, though the desk was still present, the glass was gone, and a nurse stationed by the door provided triage. Three patients stood in a line ahead of Gray, waiting for the nurse's attention. He reckoned it wouldn't be long. He glanced around, taking in his surroundings properly. He didn't like the new look. It was too bold.

It actually took five minutes for the people to be dealt with. Meanwhile more walk-ins arrived and stood behind Gray. Two of the queue in front ended up in the seating area, the third, the man with the bleeding head, was taken straight through wooden doors and into the A&E suite to Gray's right. Finally, he reached the front. The uniformed nurse, a dark-haired woman with pale skin and brown eyes focused on him, her expression neutral.

Gray showed his warrant card. "I'm here to see Doctor Maltby."

"Talk to reception, please." The nurse hiked a thumb over her shoulder, shifted her focus to the mother and child behind him. If he'd realised, Gray could have saved himself the effort of standing around in the queue.

At reception Gray repeated his request, presented his warrant card once more.

"What is it about?" asked the receptionist. Her accent was Eastern European. Gray had no idea what country she hailed from. They all sounded the same to him. Her face was pockmarked with acne scars, her hair bi-coloured – the tips dyed red.

"Police business." About as generic as you could get.

"One moment." The receptionist picked up an internal phone, tapped in a few numbers. He wondered why she'd bothered asking.

"Doctor, there is a policeman here to see you." She paused. "No, I do not know what it is about." Pause. "He just said police business." She listened again. "Okay. Doctor Maltby will be available in a few minutes, if you go to the door on the right," she pointed, "I will meet you there."

"Thanks." But she was already up and turning away.

Gray pulled at the door; however it was didn't budge. There was a click and the receptionist pushed the door open. A magnetic lock, then. Gray passed through. Within was a well-lit area, white painted walls, beds behind green curtains, lots of medical machinery and uniformed staff moving about with purpose.

He was led through the first room into a second, narrower area. More medical devices, a couple of computers at a workstation, several further beds in a row behind curtains. Standing in the centre was a woman in a white lab coat, an expression of concentration on her face. Her blonde hair was tied up and held in place by a large plastic grip. She wore no make-up, no jewelry. She stared at a document in her hands.

"This is Doctor Maltby," said the receptionist then left. Maltby shifted her focus away from the paper.

"You seem surprised," said Dr Maltby.

"You're not what I expected." Gray blinked. "I understood you were male."

Maltby laughed, revealing slightly crooked teeth. "As you can see, I'm absolutely not." She held out a hand for Gray to shake. Her grip was strong. "How can I help?"

"We received a call earlier from you reporting a nasty dog bite."

Maltby pursed her lips. "Now you have my attention. Perhaps we should go somewhere more private and talk properly." She led Gray into a small room nearby and closed the door. She put the document down on a table and crossed her arms. "It wasn't me who called you."

"Then who did?"

"One of my colleagues, I would assume."

"Why pretend to be you?"

She sighed. "Fear of reprisal, perhaps."

"I don't understand."

"It's these latest proposals by the Government, they have people rattled. If a law compelling medical professionals to report any incidents resulting from violent crime does pass then it puts at risk the Hippocratic Oath we all took."

"That's one way of looking at it." But not the only one. "The objective is to tackle the knife epidemic."

"I know."

"And it wouldn't just affect the medical profession. Anyone in public service would be duty bound. Charities too."

"It's ridiculous. How are we supposed to be held responsible for this stuff, isn't that your job?"

"Yes, however, we can't be everywhere these days." There just weren't enough cops anymore. 10,000 officers lost in the last five years.

"The staff is upset about it all to be honest."

"But it's just a suggestion right now."

"Agreed. Though we could be prosecuted if we don't report issues which subsequently come to light."

The concern seemed somewhat excessive to Gray. "And if a new law helped even just a single child that wouldn't have been helped previously doesn't that make it worthwhile?"

"Yes, of course."

"And Governments never move quickly. By the time a law came into force it might barely resemble the original plan."

Maltby raised her hands in surrender, waved Gray's arguments away. "Anyway, I was simply explaining why someone may have impersonated me."

"So, what about this dog bite?"

"There's little I can say beyond he was a teenager and pretty badly roughed up. He came in through the front entrance, meaning he hadn't called an ambulance. He had bite marks on his arms and legs. The wounds weren't fresh, probably a couple of days old. I patched him up."

"Where is he now? I'd like to speak with him."

"Against my advice, he discharged himself. He was really reluctant to be here. He only came in because the cuts got infected."

"What was his name?"

"I don't know, I'm afraid."

"If there's a dangerous dog out there and it attacks another child how would you feel, Doctor Maltby?"

"That's not fair." Gray shrugged. "Anyway, I don't think it was a stray. The lad said the dog had been set on him by somebody, deliberately."

"Deliberately?"

"That's what he told me. And he didn't give me his name. It's not a necessity to obtain treatment. This is a hospital."

"What time did he arrive?"

"Midway through my shift, say around 10am."

"Can you describe him?"

"Ginger hair, average height, freckles." Maltby's mobile bleeped. She checked the message. "Look, I really must be getting back to work. I've spent more than enough time on this."

"Is there anything else you can say?"

"I don't think so."

"The caller led us to believe this is the second attack you've had in during the week."

"I'm not aware of another, Inspector. Although it sometimes feels as if I work 24/7, I actually don't." Maltby went to the door, opened it. "I'll show you back to reception."

GRAY STOOD OUTSIDE the A&E entrance. The glass doors slid closed behind him, then parted again as he was within range of the sensor. He moved out of the way. While he was inside it had begun to rain lightly. He remembered the taxi which had pulled up as he was arriving. Everybody who entered A&E had to do so through here.

Above Gray the lens of a CCTV camera stared down at him. Somewhere within the depths of the hospital the footage would have been captured and stored. Gray just had to find out where.

It took him a couple of questions of the staff before he found the place. The security suite was located in the estate offices, to the south of the site, beneath a chimney which towered over the building.

Gray handed over his warrant card once more. The rail thin security guard stood up from the desk where he was sitting, a good six inches taller than Gray. "Ray Pickersgill," he said, "a proud Yorkshireman." Like that was very important. "What can I do for you, son?" Gray reckoned they were about the same age.

"I'd like to access your CCTV footage. Specifically, the camera over A&E at about 10am this morning." Maltby had at least told Gray what time the kid had arrived.

He stared at Gray a long moment. "I assume you've got a warrant?"

"I don't."

"Then I'm afraid I can't do anything for you, officer."

"Look..."

Pickersgill broke into laughter. "You should see your face, Inspector Gray! Of course, I'll help. I'm just joking with you. It's a Yorkshire thing."

"I'm cracking up inside," lied Gray.

"Come on through." Pickersgill crooked a finger. He led Gray into a small room dominated by a bank of screens. "We'll have to be fast, though. I'm due to finish my shift soon. I've a meeting this evening."

Pickersgill clearly wanted to be asked about it. "Meeting?"

"Alcoholics Anonymous." He burst out laughing. "Just joking! Model train club."

"Sounds exciting."

"Why do you think I tell people I go to AA?" Pickersgill sat. "10am you said?"

"That's right."

He leaned over the controls, focused on the feed he wanted and wound back the recording to 9.30am. "Just to be on the safe side," before allowing the recording to play. "Who are you looking for?"

"Male, mid-teens, ginger haired."

"Not much, but it's better than nothing. And ginger, the poor sod."

Pickersgill ran the footage. Patients turned up regularly, but after nearly a quarter of an hour and a couple of hours of elapsed footage nobody matching Maltby's description had walked through the doors. Pickersgill checked his watch. "I'm done in a few minutes and there's no overtime. They don't pay me enough to get my time for free. Can you come back tomorrow?"

"Really?"

Pickersgill laughed once more. "How about I transfer the recording onto a USB stick?"

"That works for me," said Gray through gritted teeth.

"I'll download the last twenty-four hours, then you're covered."

"Wonderful."

Pickersgill rooted around in a desk drawer, pulling out paperwork, Sellotape, pens and a stapler before he brandished a stick at Gray and grinned, like it was some trophy. Pickersgill slid the USB into a port on the front of the computer, dragged and dropped the file, waited for the transfer before ejecting the stick and handing it to Gray. "I hope you track down what you want."

"Me too."

"I'll come and find you if I get a parking ticket or something. To repay the favour, like."

"You can try."

Pickersgill laughed. "Just—"

"Joking," cut in Gray. "I know. Enjoy your train spotting."

"It's construction, Inspector."

Outside, Gray slid the stick into his pocket then made his way back across the hospital complex to his car, jacket collar turned up against the winter weather.

"Railway models, Jesus."

Seven

Gray lived on the fourth floor of an apartment block in Broadstairs above Louisa Bay. He had a sea view and no garden, two bedrooms in case anybody wanted to visit (which happened only rarely) and an allocated parking space underground.

He sat at the dining table, that was never used for such, in front of his laptop and sipped a cup of tea. He liked it hot. In the past he'd have drunk an espresso, but the caffeine kick kept him awake these days. He skipped through the footage Pickersgill had handed over. Eventually, with the time stamp saying 11.39, Gray found what he wanted.

The overhead shot showed a ginger-haired youth getting out of a taxi. A few moments later a woman carrying a toddler got out too before they walked inside. He seemed unmarked. No blood, no torn clothes, but he moved with difficulty, hobbling. Gray didn't recognise him.

Later in the morning, at 2.03am, the same kid came out of the hospital, accompanied by the same woman moving with the same difficulty. Now there were bandages on his arms, sleeves rolled up. They waited for a few minutes, the kid leaning against the wall, before a taxi turned up. All the while he appeared furtive, constantly casting glances in each direction. He checked his phone, tapping on the screen several times before putting it away.

Gray made a note of the vehicle licence numbers before he shut down the laptop. Tomorrow he'd find out where the passenger had been picked up and run the kid's face to see if they got any hits on his identity.

Gray's mobile rang. He didn't recognise the number, answered anyway.

"Inspector Gray?" A woman's voice.

"Yes."

"Hi, it's Polly Draper. From St. Peter's." He wasn't about to forget any time soon. "I've got a bit of a problem. With Mack. Mum's wire fox." A pause. "The dog."

"Oh. What's the issue?"

"It isn't Mack specifically. Well, it is."

"You're not making a great deal of sense, Mrs Draper."

"Okay, that constable of yours, who was sat with us when you came into the kitchen?"

"Worthington?"

"Yes, him. After you left he tried to kick Mack. He denied it, of course, but I saw him do it."

"Is Mack okay?"

"Fortunately, he dodged out of the way. I don't think that kind of behaviour is acceptable."

"I agree and I'll have a talk with DC Worthington in the morning."

"Thank you, I'm not keen on people who are cruel to animals. I think it shows a weak side."

"I couldn't agree more."

"You don't though. Seem harsh, that is."

"I try not to be." Except for when it came to Worthington.

"Good, Mack should be with someone who cares about him."

"I can understand that."

"I need to home him somewhere. Mum's house on his own isn't an option. Philip hates Mack and I've got children so I don't have the time for Mack; he can't stay with me."

"Do you need the name of a shelter or something?"

"That's the last thing Mum would have wanted."

"Then I don't understand."

"He liked you. Normally he's quite standoffish, doesn't enjoy people's company." Gray got that, he didn't either. "But he was different with you."

"Maybe I am a dog whisperer after all."

Draper didn't laugh, but to be fair it was a poor joke. She said, "So, I wanted to see if you'd have him."

"Have him?"

"Like look after him. Permanently."

"I'm flattered, but I can't."

"Are you sure?"

"I've never owned a dog so I wouldn't know where to start. And I live in an apartment without a garden."

"Oh, that's a shame."

"Sorry, I hope you find a good home for him."

"Me too." And then Draper was gone.

Gray was still holding his phone when it rang again. "Inspector Gray? It's Doctor Maltby from A&E. Apologies for calling so late."

"No problem. How can I help?"

"When you were here you mentioned a second dog attack. I've been asking around; it seems you were right. Somebody else was in a week or two ago. I was on holiday so didn't see them, but a colleague did."

"Do you have any details?"

"Like my patient, my colleague was extremely reluctant to talk in an official capacity. All I know is the victim was a male teenager."

Eight

Gray slept badly and woke later than usual. He grabbed a brief shower and left his flat chewing on a breakfast of plain toast. He'd run out of butter and marmite and what remained in the honey jar was mainly crumbs.

The traffic out of Broadstairs towards Margate was the usual stop / start affair. Once he hit St. Peter's Road, which ran past the edge of the graveyard and then the QEQM on the other side, the cars in front moved a little faster.

He managed to find a rare space on the road near the hospital entrance meaning avoiding paying the hospital car park fee again. While he waited for a gap to appear in the steadily flowing traffic so he could exit without getting run over, he smoothed his damp hair down with greasy fingers.

"Looking good, Sol," he said to himself in the rearview mirror.

CLOUGH PAUSED IN FRONT of spring-loaded double doors which led into the theatre. "You're aware I'll be looking to see whether the baby was murdered or not, Sol?"

"I know."

Infanticide fell under the umbrella of manslaughter and had a much shorter sentence than murder. In the early 1920s, when the law first came into force, killing a baby wasn't viewed as severely as it was now. The opinion of the time was that babies didn't suffer as much as adults. And, as babies were mouths to feed rather than a means to put food on the table, they were deemed of lesser importance to the family unit. Although the legislation had been addressed several times since, the inferior view of babies in the eyes of the law persisted for some time.

"It's just some people find this a difficult subject," said Clough.

"Parents, you mean?"

"That and, well, your situation."

Situation, an interesting way to describe Gray's past. His missing son.

"I'll be fine."

"I just wanted to make sure," said Clough.

"I appreciate it, Ben, but let's see where the evidence takes us."

Clough, apparently satisfied, used his shoulder to push his way through into the examination room then waited for Gray to pass before following, releasing the door and allowing it to swing shut.

The space was all white tiles and stainless steel, dazzling spotlights, glittering surgical instruments, and gaping drains; everything designed for an easy clean. The air was icy and stank of disinfectant.

"Good morning," said Clough to a person already in the theatre, holding a camera, there to take shots as directed for the PM report. She was small and slight – it was hard to be more specific about build because, like Clough and Gray, she wore a full-length white evidence suit, a hat over her hair and a face mask.

"This is Gill," said Clough.

For important or high-profile PMs, the examination room could have five or six people present, including the crime scene manager and other detectives. Not today.

Most pathologists employed a stenographer to take down their notes, however Clough preferred to make a verbal record on tape and transcribe the details himself. Slower, but he liked to go over his own information.

The viewing area, where Gray usually tried to witness the post-mortem (if he absolutely had to attend), was separated from Clough's workspace by a large plate-glass window. That area was plain in comparison, as if the lion's share of the budget had been reserved for the dead. The walls were washed in a lemon yellow; rows of uncomfortable chairs fixed to the floor, all facing the same direction – towards the window – making the spectacle of evisceration difficult to avoid.

The corpse, but no box, was already present. A tiny body wrapped in white, made to appear even smaller by the size of the gurney. Clough placed himself one side of the table. Gray stood opposite to get a clear view of proceedings. He shuddered and not with the cold.

"You okay, Sol?" asked Clough.

"Fine," lied Gray.

Clough turned to Gill, said, "Ready to proceed?"

"Whenever you are."

A microphone suspended from the ceiling hung near the pathologist. "Let's see what we have, shall we?" He clicked a button, turned the recording on. "The body is wrapped in what appears to be a muslin cloth." Clough gently touched the binding, pulling it back slightly. The baby's skin was brown and dry, drawn tight across the face, shrivelled and seemingly tough as leather.

"Would you mind?" asked Clough.

As she leaned in to take a couple of shots at different angles Clough explained, "Mummification occurs in hot, dry conditions like a desert. The skin dries and the tissues harden rather than putrefy, as is typical."

"We don't have deserts in this country, Ben."

"I'm aware of that. A loft or chimney would also be a suitable location, if that is the best description. Somewhere hot and draughty. The person must also be thin – they are more likely to cool and desiccate than someone larger. A baby is a perfect example. Newborns are relatively sterile so they are less susceptible to putrefaction and more to mummification under the right conditions.

Clough tried to peel back the outer white cloth.

"This is the first time I've seen a mummified baby. It used to happen a lot, apparently. Back when having a child out of wedlock was shameful. Sometimes the babies were stillborn or died soon after birth as the mother struggled alone. It was even possible for the baby to be murdered. The corpse would be hidden in the loft or beneath floorboards as burial wasn't an option."

"Good God," said Gray.

"It occurred more often than you'd think. We could conceivably be looking at somebody older than both of us." Gray was pushing fifty, Clough at least five years behind. "As social attitudes shifted mummified bodies were found less. I know my predecessor, Dr Jenkinson, assessed several cases like this. Not much bothered him, but dead babies were definitely one of his weak spots."

The outer binding wasn't coming easily. "It looks like the baby has been swaddled," said Gray. The cloth tightly wound around the youngster, keeping the arms down. He remembered doing this with his own children. At first, he'd been uncomfortable with the process, but it was supposed to calm a restless infant and tired parents will try almost anything. To his surprise it had worked.

Clough reached for a pair of scissors. Slowly he snipped the side of the cloth, along the length of the body. Eventually he was able to remove the material and place it into a clear plastic evidence bag. Beneath was a baby grow, a white one-piece full-length outfit. There was colour on the chest area. Gray got closer. "Teletubbies," he said. Four weird-looking doll-like cartoon figures of various heights, arms raised, waving and smiling.

Gill took several photos of the body from different angles, the baby grow and the Teletubbies print.

"What?" asked Clough.

"It's a kid's programme. Very popular in the '90s onwards."

"I must have missed that one."

"There could be a date on the image, from a copyright."

Clough peered closely. "You're right, there is. It says 2009. So, the child is no more than ten years old."

Clough cut the baby grow away then removed the fabric, so the baby lay naked. The clothing went into a separate evidence bag which Clough sealed. "Female," said Clough. So, Draper's guess had been correct. Gill took some photos.

The pathologist carefully lifted the baby into a set of scales and noted the weight. Next, Clough measured her length. "She'd have been quite small at birth, in the lower quartile of what was deemed healthy. Possibly she was slightly premature, or the mother was undernourished.

"The mummification process typically preserves the body beautifully." Not a word Gray would have chosen. "If there are any external injuries we should see them clearly." Clough pointed to the right side of the baby's stomach, low down above the hip. "This is where putrefaction starts, the gut is full of bacteria. When you die the bacteria exit the bowel and enter the abdominal cavity, followed by the blood vessels. The abdominal wall is close to the intestine which is why we typically see it here as a green mark, like a stain but," Clough leaned in, scanned the torso, "I can't see anything." Neither could Gray, but it wasn't his place to say.

Clough bent right down to painstakingly examine the body, pausing periodically for photographs. He carefully lifted and turned the child over, checking every inch of the tiny corpse. Eventually he straightened and said, "No obvious signs of bruising or any marks at all. There's some mould." Clough pointed to a white mark on the baby's back. "But that's not unusual. Attack by pests hasn't occurred. Sometimes beetles and moths get their mouths in."

"Let's be thankful for small mercies," said Gray, the image of feasting bugs stark in his mind.

"Time to go inside." Clough lifted a scalpel. Gray didn't feel too good. "First, we've got to determine whether the baby had lived at all – no life, then no death." One breath and the baby would have been deemed to have survived the birth, then manslaughter or murder could be considered. But if the baby hadn't lived then it couldn't be killed. "As much as is feasible, of course, given the state of the body," said Clough. "If the baby expired in the womb the corpse would show early decomposition, the mummification makes it impossible to know that now. So, I'll have to examine the skull."

Clough sliced into the leathery skin. Gray couldn't look, even just the sound was enough to put his teeth on edge. Eventually Clough said, "The skull seems fine, perfectly normal. The bones are aligned. A death early in the pregnancy would result in the plates overlapping or collapsing. No sign of that." Throughout the process Gill had been snapping photographs, seemingly unaffected. Not so for Gray.

"You all right, Sol?" asked Clough again. Gray held up a hand. If he opened his mouth, he felt like he'd throw up. "I'll continue then."

Gray glanced over. The pathologist turned his attention to the chest cavity. Gray dry swallowed, trying to force down the pressure building in his throat and set his eyes on the nearest white-tiled wall.

Again, the separation of the dried skin, then the whirring of a saw followed by a sharp clicking, like the sound of breaking chicken bones.

"Hmm, the lungs are like dried, shrivelled prunes," said Clough.

Gray could stand no more and he marched out of the theatre to get some fresh air.

A HALF HOUR OR SO LATER Clough entered the office. Gray was seated. "Sorry about that," he said.

"Not your fault," replied Clough. "Sometimes I forget others don't view a body the same way I do. You're feeling all right now, I hope?"

"Better. How do you do that? Every day, cut up cadavers?"

"I find the human body fascinating." Clough sat behind his desk. "I take it as a privilege to be able to understand what happened to people and give their relatives an explanation. Sometimes its closure for them."

"We don't know who the girl is."

"We don't know *yet*, Sol. But I'm sure you will find out soon."

"I'll do my best." Gray sighed. "Anyway, what else did you find?"

"I've sent off some samples for toxicological, bacterial and viral checks. At the moment I'd say there are several potential causes of death. Maybe a bacterial infection, or shaken baby syndrome, abusive head trauma as it's called these days, but it's impossible to tell because of the condition of the brain. Or SIDS – sudden infant death syndrome."

"SIDS is when there's no obvious cause of death, right?"

"No obvious *unnatural* cause of death. Back in the 80s and 90s SIDS was statistically significant, but it's been in decline for years since awareness of the actual basis for the event has increased."

"I remember," said Gray. "Not putting the baby face down, no smoking in the house, keep the room temperature Goldilocks." It had been a major worry for Gray and his wife.

He remembered checking on both his kids constantly and monitoring a thermometer to ensure they didn't overheat.

"Goldilocks?"

"Not too hot, not too cold but just right."

"Is that some joke between parents?"

"No, just me and Kate."

"Oh, sorry."

"My fault, not yours. Go on."

"Anyway, pathologists got into the habit of presuming SIDS so it became a catch all. We're better now. Until I get back the results from the analyses, I'll be marking cause of death as unascertained."

"Okay, thanks Ben."

"If I receive any further pertinent data, I'll give you an update." Gray stood. "By the way, have you heard about Amos Jenkinson?"

Jenkinson was Clough's predecessor and someone Gray had worked with for years until his retirement. Gray said, "Last I was aware he was struggling with Alzheimer's. That was at least a year ago, maybe more." Gray hadn't had any contact with Jenkinson for a while, not since a cold case took him to the retired pathologist's house in Fordwich. Once that disease took hold, there was no getting free. It was like a black hole, sucking every brain function into the irrecoverable depths. His daughter, Fiona, had been caring for him. Gray didn't know her well; Jenkinson had kept home and work life separate.

"He's got cancer now, terminal apparently. He's weeks, maybe even just days left."

"Good God."

"I only learned from a colleague."

"I'll give Fiona a call." He still had her number in his phone.

"I'd have thought she'd have told me herself," said Clough.

"Do you two know each other?"

"Once, years back. Anyway," Clough forced a smile. "Good luck tracing the baby's parents."

Gray left Clough's office and made his way through the hospital. Once he was in the car park he rang Fiona.

She answered. "Hello?"

"Fiona, its Solomon Gray. I've just heard about your father. I'm really sorry."

Fiona sighed heavily down the speaker. "Thanks for getting in touch. The Alzheimer's has got a lot worse since you were last here. He barely remembers anything these days."

"How are you coping?"

"It's not easy. Bits of him are starting to shut down. He can't walk as well as he used to. It's as if his brain is forgetting how to carry out subconscious functions."

"God, that's awful."

"I'm glad you rang. I've been struggling to contact everyone given how much has been going on. A couple of days ago I learned that Dad's bowel cancer had returned. There was no point telling him, of course, he'd have no memory of the conversation a minute later. Frankly, it might be for the best."

"Ben said he doesn't have much time left."

"Not Ben Clough?"

"Yes."

"Oh."

"Is that a problem? We weren't gossiping."

"No, no it's fine. I'm glad he did. We haven't spoken for ages. It's just a surprise to hear his name is all. If you want to come over and see Dad one last time, this is it."

"Maybe." Gray had seen how dementia and cancer ravaged people. Two of his grandparents had suffered. He reached his car.

"I wouldn't blame you at all if you just want to remember him how he was and didn't visit. Dad's barely the person he was."

Now Gray felt guilty. Jenkinson wouldn't be aware of Gray, but Fiona would. "No, I'll definitely be there soon."

"That would be great, thanks Sol." Gray could hear the relief in her voice. "Don't leave it long, though."

Nine

Gray headed over to Pfeffer's desk and passed her the USB stick that Pickersgill had given him yesterday with the A&E CCTV footage on. "Can you pull an image off here please, and run an ID check. The time is 11.39am, male, ginger, young. He's getting out of a taxi. Also, run the plate and talk to the firm, find out where the kid was picked up? And check social media, he's more than likely to have something like a Facebook account."

"Who are we talking about here?" asked Pfeffer as she took the stick.

"Sorry." Gray's mind was still on the baby and Jenkinson. "This is the kid who was reported as being attacked by the dog."

"Okay, makes sense now. I'll get right on it."

Worthington was noisily clanking a teaspoon in a mug of something hot in the kitchen area. Gray went over. The Geordie didn't bother to offer Gray anything.

"A word, please," said Gray.

"Sure."

"In my office."

"Ah." Worthington pushed off.

"Do you want me at all, sir?" Ibbotson asked as they passed by him.

"Did I ask you, Ted?"

"No, sir."

"There you go then."

Gray closed the door. Worthington remained standing, blew on the surface of his drink, not looking at Gray. "What's this about?"

"St. Peter's yesterday."

"Ibbotson told me what you said. I'll be a good boy from now on." He turned to leave.

"It's not that."

Worthington turned back, gave Gray an unimpressed stare like his teenage daughter used to, years ago. Surly, disrespectful. "Can't wait to hear what, then."

"I had a call from Mrs Draper. She claimed you tried to kick her dog."

"That's an exaggeration. He was attempting to hump my leg, so I shook him away."

"She says differently."

"Were you there? Did you see it? No, you didn't. Therefore, it's her word against mine."

"I don't believe you."

"Got proof?" Gray didn't answer. "That's what I thought." Suddenly, Worthington grinned. "If that's everything, sir, I'll get back to my desk." He walked out, leaving the door open.

Gray flopped into his chair, faced the wall, his back to the detective's office. His phone bleeped. A text telling him he had voicemail. "Inspector Gray, Alexander Vardie of Social Services returning your call. Please ring me back when you're free."

Gray found Vardie's number in his recents list, stored it, dialed but got his voicemail. "And this is Inspector Gray, trying to contact you again." After breaking the connection he returned his attention to the PNC, searched for any dog related incidents in Thanet.

Nothing.

"There you are, Sol." Bethany Underwood, standing at Gray's door. "Have you got five minutes?"

"Sure," said Gray, attempting to sound mildly pleased to see her. It was maybe three months since they'd last spoken. He hadn't even known she was pregnant until after she'd gone to take the time off.

He knew Underwood as slim, verging on that bit too skinny, with frizzy, bleach blonde hair and a nervous disposition. Her nails were bitten to the quick and she furiously smoked whenever she took a break.

Seemingly, not anymore.

Underwood appeared relaxed and happy, a grin on her face, something he struggled to remember previously. Her hair was straight and brown now – the artificial attack by chemicals seemingly now done with. Underwood closed Gray's door and sat.

"Congratulations," said Gray. "How are you?"

"I'm great," said Underwood, "she's great." Must be a daughter then. Another fact he wasn't aware of. Underwood pulled out a photo, passed it to Gray. Yes, an infant. Dressed in pink.

"What's her name?"

"Amelie."

"Nice. And you're looking well."

"It's been a revelation. Caring for something so helpless, it really brings everything else into perspective." She shook her head. "Some of the stuff I was worrying about, God, ridiculous.

And we're getting married soon." Underwood held out her left hand, displayed a ring with a sparkly stone. "You must come to the wedding."

"I'd be delighted." Actually, he couldn't think of anything worse. Milling around with people he didn't know, making small talk, watching others get steadily drunk.

"The invite is in the post, then."

"Look forward to it."

"And I'll be expecting you to bring someone."

Gray forced a laugh. "I can't think of anybody who'd want to be my date." He moved the subject on quickly. "DCI Hamson said you'd want to discuss the baby in the box."

Underwood scrunched up her face, like she'd tasted something bitter. "How could somebody do that?"

"We don't know all the circumstances."

"Even so." Gray wondered how much Underwood would have been bothered before she'd given birth herself. She continued, "I'm getting an increasing number of calls from the press. They're really interested. One of the bastards described it as a bit of light relief after the Brexit shambles."

"Nice."

"I told him what I thought, don't you worry. Anyway, there's a hunger for information on the topic. I expect we'll see reporters here in Margate before long. Then they'll work out where the house is, who the relatives are, where they live. Speaking of the relatives, what do you think their reaction will be?"

"Polly Draper and Philip Ogilvy? Hard to say, I've only met them once." Underwood waited for Gray to consider. "I suspect Ogilvy would probably get aggressive, but hard to say with Draper."

"Maybe I should advise them as to what they might expect?"

"Probably sensible. I've got a contact number for the daughter. She might give you her brother's details."

"What about a press conference?"

"There's not much we can say right now."

"When we've more detail, then."

"I'm not keen." Gray didn't like being the centre of attention in front of the press in such a false environment.

"The leeches will keep sucking 'til they find blood."

"I can't help that, Bethany."

"Don't say I didn't warn you." She stood. "Can I have the number for Draper?"

"No problem." Gray scrolled through the contacts in his phone, wrote the details down and handed them over. And then she was gone.

Gray's phone bleeped. A text, from Fiona Jenkinson. "Do you still want to come over and see Dad? I understand if you don't."

Gray replied, "This evening okay?"

Fiona's response came back within seconds. "Great."

A knock at his door. Pfeffer. "I've got an identity on the ginger kid who went to A&E," she said. "Freddie Kirton."

"Don't know him."

"He's from Newington." A council estate the far side of Ramsgate, a well-known trouble spot. "He's fifteen and has a couple of ASBOs to his name."

"And someone set a dog on him."

"Maybe it was a falling out between scally mates?"

"Possibly. I'll find out when I talk to him."

KIRTON LIVED ON AUCKLAND Avenue, in the shadow of Staner Court, a high rise on the southern edge of the estate. His house was an unimaginatively designed red brick semi. Hard edges, sharp angles, uPVC windows. Opposite stood the Newington Community Centre, a single-storey white-painted building, and beyond that was a play area with swings and a roundabout.

Three kids on bikes, on the grass behind the community centre, watched Gray park. He eyeballed them as he got out of the car. The kids returned the stare, didn't move. Gray walked up to the house, stepping over children's brightly coloured plastic toys strewn on the driveway. He knocked on the door, glanced over his shoulder. The kids were still there.

No answer so Gray tried again. Now the door opened. A woman with a child, maybe under two years old, on her hip. She wore dark blue tracksuit bottoms and a white sleeveless t-shirt revealing a small tattoo on her shoulder; a couple of Chinese or Japanese symbols Gray couldn't translate. Her mousy brown hair was held up by a plastic grip. This was the woman from the CCTV footage. He was in the right place.

"Yes?" she said.

"I'd like to speak with Freddie Kirton."

"Why?" Gray showed his warrant card. She leant over, read the card closely. "What's he supposed to have done?"

"I just want a talk with him. About his visit to the hospital yesterday."

The woman blinked. The child stuffed a thumb into his mouth. "He won't tell you anything." She glanced past Gray to the kids on their bikes. "Nobody does."

"I'd like to try anyway."

"He's in his bedroom." She moved out of his way, allowed Gray to enter then pushed the door shut with her foot. "Second door on the left. When you're done come and find me in the kitchen."

"Okay."

"Freddie!" she shouted. "There's someone here to see you."

Gray passed by a buggy before heading up the stairs. He found Kirton propped up in bed, a pillow behind him. The walls were covered in posters – for games and movies, all sci-fi like Star Trek, Star Wars and Fortnite.

Kirton's hair was a strong copper colour and unkempt. Skinny too. He wore a short-sleeved shirt, bandages on show. The room was hot despite the winter weather outside. Kirton was intent upon some shoot-em-up console game. His tongue poked out the side of his mouth while a thumb rattled fast onto a controller button.

Gray waited for a few seconds, but the kid didn't divert his attention away from the exploding aliens. "Freddie."

"What?"

"I'm here about the dog." Gray held out his warrant card. Now Kirton properly looked at Gray, stopped hammering the button. A scream emitted from the TV. Kirton's character had died. He pressed another button and the game paused.

"I don't know what you're talking about." Kirton absently rubbed a large white spot on his chin.

"You went into hospital yesterday with bite marks on you. They'd got infected. I spoke to the doctor who treated you." Kirton's fingers moved from his face to the bandages. He said nothing, stared at Gray. "Somebody set a dog on you."

"That's not what happened. I climbed over a fence and there was a dog in the garden. It went for me. It was all my fault."

"Where was this?"

"Other side of the estate." Kirton wave his hand towards the window. "I don't remember exactly."

"You don't remember where a dog bit you?"

"On the leg and arm." Kirton rolled up his sleeve to show Gray a white bandage.

"I meant the address."

"Oh, no." Kirton shrugged. "And it weren't really like what you said. He were just playing, jumping up at me. No biggie." He picked up his controller, began shooting again.

"Freddie?" asked Gray but Kirton paid him no attention.

Gray headed downstairs. The kitchen door stood open. Gray glanced inside. The woman was on her own, seated at a table. "I've just put him down for a sleep." She meant the toddler. "Did he talk?"

"Not really. Just that he'd been jumped at by a dog, and it was his fault. He totally played it down."

The woman beckoned Gray. She closed the door behind him. "I'm Laura, by the way, his step mum. He tells me stuff 'cos he thinks I'm more of a mate than a parent. He's a good kid, you know."

"He seems all right." From what Gray could tell inside a couple of minutes.

"Every now and again he loses control, it's the ADHD." Gray had heard a lot about this condition in recent years, never anything previously. He half wondered sometimes if it was actually real, or some invented behaviour.

"When was he attacked?" asked Gray.

"A couple of days ago. He was in a right state. His clothes had been shredded, there was blood all over him. He was really upset. Scratches everywhere and a couple of bite marks. I wanted him to go to the hospital, but he wouldn't have it. His Dad agreed so we put him to bed. Little I can say, right? As he's not mine. All I could do was clean him up as best I could.

"When I went in to check on him later, I asked what happened. Some man had gone for him. Came out of nowhere, knocked Freddie to the floor. He held a dog on a chain. The man let the animal snap and growl at Freddie, getting closer and closer. Freddie was utterly terrified."

"Did the man say anything?"

"Just that Freddie better behave, not get into any more trouble. But that's what's strange, he hasn't been doing anything. As I said, he's a decent kid."

"What did the man look like?"

"Freddie couldn't say anything beyond he was big and had a scarf across his face."

"Hair colour?"

"He wore a hat."

"Where was Freddie attacked?"

"There's a footpath near St. Christopher's Church that connects Princess Margaret Avenue and Rockstone Way." Gray didn't know it. "He had to walk home, bleeding. Everybody would have seen it."

"I'm sorry to hear that."

"I only took him into hospital because the cuts got infected. When we got back there was a box on the doorstep. Inside was a brand new games console and a note addressed to Freddie."

"What did it say?"

"Just 'Sorry'. Don't you think that's strange?" The child began to cry in the background, distracting Laura. "I'd better go to him."

"Have you heard of any other kids being mauled?" The baby was still crying. Laura shook her head. "Thanks for your help. I'll see myself out."

Gray sat in his car. The kids were gone. He looked up St. Christopher's Church on his phone's map app. Just over half a mile away and opposite the Marlowe school, one of the government's much touted academies. As Gray drove off he glanced up at Kirton's window. The kid was watching him from the shadows.

THE FOOTPATH WAS ON the curved corner of Princess Margaret Avenue, a strangely designed road in the shape of a cucumber with a narrow patch of grass in the centre separating the two halves.

Houses stood one side of the narrow path, maybe a hundred yards long, fenced-in church grounds the other. The building itself was comparatively new, built in a red brick, regular design which Gray would never have guessed was a place of worship.

He paused on Rockstone Way. More semi-detached houses set back from the road behind small front gardens. Nothing remarkable. Gray returned the way he'd come, slowly now, his eyes on the ground. He didn't see anything notable, just chewing gum patches and dog shit. He glanced over the fence into people's gardens. No animals in sight.

He stopped halfway along. Bushes and trees hung low over the path both directions. He couldn't see the exits. Would people have come running if they heard someone scream? A dog snarling, barking? Maybe not. Bystanders tended to be just that – generally not interested in the pain of others.

Gray's phone rang as he neared his car. "Inspector Gray, this is Alexander Vardie of Social Services. I understand you've been trying to reach me."

"Yes, sir. I wanted to take up some of your time to discuss one of your foster carers."

"Why, specifically?"

"It's better we speak face to face."

"When were you thinking of?"

"As soon as possible, this afternoon if that's feasible."

Vardie made a long hmm sound before saying, "I'm sorry, I'm tied up all day."

"When is a good time?"

"I'm afraid I'm really busy."

"This is a serious case, sir."

"As is mine, inspector. I'm currently on the other side of Kent dealing with a major issue and I won't be back for a while."

"Please make yourself available when possible, Mr Vardie."

"Is it a matter of life or death, Inspector Gray?"

"No," admitted Gray.

"I might be back in two days if that works?"

It would have to. "When?"

"At the moment I can't be specific. Let me call you, all right?"

Again, Gray didn't really have any choice. "Okay."

"I've got your number so I'll ring when I can." And then Vardie was gone.

Ten

Amos Jenkinson had retired several years ago to a barn conversion nestled in the village of Fordwich, just off the Canterbury road. A couple of thousand years back Fordwich was a major port, but the gradual silting up of the River Stour meant it was now landlocked. Jenkinson's home was on the edge of the community, at the end of a cul-de-sac with fields to the rear. Gray parked on the drive behind a small red Fiat.

He rang the bell. The traffic making its way in and out of the city was audible. Fiona opened up. She'd lost weight since the last time Gray had seen her. Her hair was shorter, cut to the nape of her neck, and entirely silvered. There were dark circles under bloodshot eyes. She'd dressed plainly, in jeans and a baggy black sweatshirt. "Sol." She made a weak attempt at a smile. "Come in." Fiona stepped out of the way.

The kitchen was along a corridor at the rear, overlooking the once neat garden. The grass was long now and the bushes unruly. Dark brown leaves lay spread over the lawn, deposited from the branches of an overhanging tree.

"Do you want anything?" asked Fiona. "I haven't much in I'm afraid. I can stretch to a cup of tea."

"I'm fine, thanks."

"Take a seat." She pointed to a high stool at a breakfast bar and began filling a kettle at the sink.

"How's your Dad?"

"His mind is completely gone, and the body is barely clinging on." She switched the kettle on. "I'm really sorry, but he's asleep at the moment. You may have wasted your time coming over."

Gray was actually relieved. "Really, it's no problem."

"I'm glad you did as it's nice to see a friendly face. And a famous face."

"Famous?"

"You're in the papers. The baby in the box."

"God, that."

"It must have been horrible. I knew Andrea Ogilvy, by the way."

"Oh?"

"I work for Thanet Social Services. Right now, I'm on leave, of course, while I care for Dad. I met Andrea several times through my job. I work with vulnerable families. Sometimes it's necessary to rehouse the children to get them out of potentially difficult circumstances, even if just overnight. Andrea was one of the people I'd go to for fostering."

"What was she like?"

"One of the most caring people I ever met. Always there for everyone."

"How often did you see her?"

Fiona shrugged. "It really varied. Sometimes several times a week, then not for months. There was no telling."

"When did you last see her?"

"On the day of her retirement, eight years ago. That was something else I thought never she'd stop; looking after children."

"Why did she?"

"I think the joy went out of it after her husband died." Fiona shook her head. "How did she die?"

"I'm not sure, old age, I think. There was nothing suspicious."

"I thought Andrea would outlive us all. She was so strong and full of energy." Fiona rubbed a hand across her face. "What with Dad's illness, I've been so cut off lately I rarely hear any news. I thought one of my colleagues would have told me. I'm really pissed off they haven't."

"Maybe they're busy too."

"Maybe. What about the baby, has she been identified?"

"Not at the moment. I've spoken to Polly and Philip. It's a mystery to them. They told me that children and sometimes babies were brought round at all times of day and night. So, it could be one of these. At this stage we just don't have enough information."

"Children are separated from parents only when it's absolutely necessary and after a lot of consultation and risk assessment and lots and lots of meetings. When it comes to kids nothing happens lightly."

"I'm sure."

"It's simply that whenever tragic situations occur, it's always the social worker who gets it in the neck."

"I'm not here to criticise."

"Sorry." Fiona pinched the bridge of her nose. "It's been very stressful lately."

"Would you fix my hair?" The tone was gravelly and quivered. Fiona glanced over Gray's shoulder.

In the doorway stood Amos Jenkinson. He was frail, bent at the waist and using a metal framed walker to keep himself upright. His wrinkled clothes hung off him. His cheeks were hollow, eyes sunken, skin wrinkled like a chicken's. Jenkinson still sported the over-sized, pork-chop sideburns but his hair was long and grey and there was stubble now. In his hand he held a hairbrush.

"Who are you?"

"Dad, it's all right. This is an old friend of yours."

Jenkinson fixed his eyes on Gray. "Who are you?!"

Gray held his hand out, walked towards Jenkinson. "It's me, Solomon."

"Don't," said Fiona to Gray.

Jenkinson backed up, his mouth working. He dropped the brush. "Go away, leave me alone!" Then he fell over and shrieked.

"Dad!" Fiona pushed past Gray and ran to her father, who'd rolled over onto his knees. Gray tried to help but Jenkinson was crawling along the floor like a baby. "Leave me alone!"

"I'll deal with him," said Fiona and pushed the door closed.

Gray picked up the brush from where it had fallen and waited. Fiona returned in a couple of minutes. He said, "I'm sorry about that." He held out the brush and Fiona took it.

"It's not your fault. I've given him something to calm down. God, I need a drink." Fiona went to a cupboard, pulled out a bottle and a glass. She poured herself a shot of vodka, her hand shaking. "He's not always like that." Gulped a shot down. "Some days he's worse." Fiona smiled, like it was a bad joke. She rolled up her shirt sleeve. There was a fresh scratch along her arm, like fingernails had dragged. Above, yellowing bruises circling her arm.

"Do you need help?"

"I can't put him into a home, Sol. Not now. There's not long left. Every day I can have with him, even if it's like this."

"I'm not sure how you cope."

"Sometimes we get what we deserve."

"I'd better be going."

"I'll walk you out." On the way they passed a bathroom, the door open. Fiona put the brush onto the sink before she opened the front door for him.

"Call me if I can help."

Fiona closed the door on Gray as her father started shouted obscenities.

Gray sat in his car, key in the ignition. Seeing Jenkinson so withered hit him hard. He was starting to feel old. Time was racing, pushing him along at a seemingly faster and faster rate. Twenty years ago, it had been weddings and christenings – new beginnings. Now, it was significant birthday parties, retirements and divorces. All too soon it would be funerals. People he'd worked with for years were starting to disappear, new faces joining the team. People he was aloof from because of the age gap, which was developing into a chasm. He struggled to relate to people anyway, without the intervening generational aspect and his seniority. Like Pfeffer, she was decades younger.

Then he remembered the baby. She hadn't had a chance to age.

Gray's phone rang. "It's Alexander Vardie. My trip is ending earlier than expected. Can we get together at my office? 9am tomorrow morning? If you're still interested in meeting, of course?"

"I'll be there."

"Great, see you then." Vardie cut the call.

Gray twisted the key and the engine started. He headed home, hoping he was going to start getting some answers soon.

Eleven

Kent County Council Social Services was situated in an unusual location – down a dead-end street on an industrial estate on the edge of Broadstairs. To one side of the government building stood an auto garage and opposite an indoor skatepark.

The building itself was anonymous, no signs out front. The central and main portion was two storeys of grey concrete in the art deco style, flanked by more modern breezeblock wings clad in maroon-coloured corrugated metal on the upper floor. Cars were shoved all around the building but Gray found an empty visitor's spot right out front. The entrance was a single door which led to a lobby as undistinguished as the exterior.

"Inspector Gray, I'm here to see Alexander Vardie," Gray told the receptionist, a middle-aged, dark-haired Asian woman – Chinese or Japanese, Gray could never figure out the difference – wearing a headset. She nodded, prodded a button and spoke quietly into the microphone near her lips.

"He'll be with you momentarily." She pointed to a couple of chairs around a table. "You can wait over there."

"I'm fine." Gray didn't move.

Soon, a smartly dressed man, in blue suit trousers with matching waistcoat and pale blue shirt open at the neck, descended the stairs. His skin was pockmarked by old acne scars. He sported a neatly clipped goatee and moustache, the ends waxed so they pointed outwards. His brown hair was slicked back and wet-looking.

He walked towards Gray, held his hand out. "Alexander Vardie. Pleased to meet you." His grip was firm and dry, his accent London. "Will you follow me?"

Vardie led Gray back up the stairs to a plain meeting room a few yards along the blank corridor. The room was whitewashed walls and a meeting table in a pale wood. The blinds across the windows were drawn, blocking out the view. A black laptop, the lid down, sat on the table, the power light flashing steadily.

"Please, take a seat," said Vardie. Gray did so. Vardie took the place opposite, the laptop adjacent to him. "Before we start, can I see your warrant card?"

"No problem." Gray handed over the laminated sheet the size of a credit card.

Vardie examined it closely before passing it back. "Can't be too careful."

"What do you do here, Mr Vardie?"

"Me or the council?"

"Both."

"We offer social service support for a whole manner of people in a whole series of situations. From children to adults. Benefits, pensions, housing, disability and so on. And I'm what's called a Senior Practitioner. The team of Thanet-based social workers report into me. I, in turn, report to the Social Care Manager. The social workers spend most of their time in the field, working directly with the families. I'm more office based than they are. However, periodically I get out and about. Sometimes our cases may take us all across the county. Say if we're moving a family from somewhere like Tonbridge to Ramsgate."

"What about the actual fostering process?"

"There's two types – short or long term. The former typically occurs for children in case proceedings or who can't be looked after by whoever is legally responsible for them. The latter is when a child needs a more permanent home."

"How long could this care last for?"

Vardie shrugged. "It really depends. Anywhere from days to a couple of years. Every situation is different. Some are straightforward, others more complex."

"And how does a child come into your care?"

"Again, that's a very broad question and can vary drastically. At one extreme the child could be at risk and forcibly removed or, at the other end of the scale, voluntarily given up by the parent or parents. Either way, a social worker is assigned to carry out an assessment of the child's position before developing a care plan. One of the options may be long-term fostering. Another, reunification – where all parties work together to place the child back in their home. This is our preference, of course.

"If the care plan is one of reunification the care giver may spend lots of time with the birth family. Usually, new foster parents start with short-term cases to get a taste and build up experience. Ultimately, they may decide fostering isn't for them. Another outcome is the child moves onto longer term fostering, so the child stays with the initial care givers as a bridge before they find somewhere more permanent. Occasionally, children placed in short term foster care end up staying much longer." He leant forward on his forearms, interlinked his fingers. "Now, that's all rather boring. You wanted to talk about an investigation?"

"Andrea Ogilvy, I understand she was an approved foster carer?"

"Ah, yes. The shoebox baby. I rather hoped that might be the subject." Vardie sat more upright, interest on his face. "I never met Mrs Ogilvy. I only transferred down two years ago. From what I've read she was one of our general providers. This is where I'll need to refer to the records." Vardie pulled over the laptop, lifted the lid, tapped away at the keys. Presumably entering a password. He stared at the screen briefly then nodded to himself.

"Before we proceed there's one aspect I'd like to clarify, Inspector Gray. As you're probably aware there have been a number of high-profile institutional child abuse cases recently. When Mrs Ogilvy started fostering back in the '70s things would have been very different to a handful of years ago and different again now. There were far fewer checks and balances for one thing. Over time we've tightened up all of our procedures.

"Now, my management are very alert to the fact that the shoebox baby is garnering lots of media attention. So far, is your case indicating any exploitation or mishandling we need to be aware of?"

"Do you think there's been some abuse going on?"

"We don't believe there has."

"So why are you asking?"

"I'm not, management are."

"What are they worried about?"

"I can't say." Now Gray frowned. "Because they haven't told me."

"Is this going to be an issue, Mr Vardie?"

"I don't know."

Gray was tempted to push through Vardie and the over-cautious bureaucracy, but that would probably result in him having to come back again and he couldn't be bothered. Better to play the game. "To answer your first question, I don't know either. It's too early to say." Vardie grimaced. "But it doesn't seem that way right now."

Vardie flashed a relieved smile. "Good, of course we'll provide any information we possibly can. The care of the people we look after is the paramount concern."

"I'm sure," said Gray. "So, Mrs Ogilvy."

Vardie blinked. "Yes, sorry." Vardie returned his attention to the laptop. "Her record was exemplary for the majority of her time as a carer, right up until she stopped about eight years ago. The service she provided was mainly short term, with a handful of longer-term children too. Usually the subjects were of the more, uhm, challenging variety."

"One of Mrs Ogilvy's own children mentioned some issue with the council regarding an accusation."

Vardie read on before saying, "That's correct. We served Mrs Ogilvy a Section 47 Enquiry."

"What's one of those?"

"It's a formal investigation and it's instigated when, I quote, reasonable cause to suspect that a child who lives, or is found, in their area is suffering, or is likely to suffer, significant harm."

"This was a formal process, you said?"

"Correct."

"Because her daughter mentioned it was just the opposite. She played everything down."

"A sensitive subject, perhaps?"

"Maybe. It was regarding her husband, right?"

"You're well informed, Inspector. After the complaint and prior to the resolution all fostering activity at the Ogilvy's continued. The allegation was subsequently found to be unsubstantiated." Vardie scanned through the notes some more. "It seems we attempted to re-establish Mrs Ogilvy as a carer, but she declined."

"Does it say why?"

"I can't see a reason. Then again, Mrs Ogilvy was in her late 60s. It's a tiring business at the best of times."

"Can I get a copy of the Section 47 and the investigation?" Gray slid over his business card. "My email address is on there."

"I'll send it to you now; otherwise I'll get involved in something else and forget." Vardie tapped away at the keyboard, clicked the mouse a few times then said, "Done. It'll be in your inbox when you reach your office." Vardie grinned once more. "The power of the world wide web."

"Thanks."

"You're welcome. Is there anything else I can help you with?"

"Not right now."

"You've got my number, call me if you do." Vardie stood. "I'll show you out."

When Gray reached his car, his phone rang.

Pfeffer. "We've had an initial report back on the DNA analyses, sir."

Twelve

T he contact at the PFA laboratory where the DNA tests occurred was Dr Amy Aplin. Her report, of several pages in length, was awaiting Gray on email when he arrived back at the station. He opened the DNA report and glanced over the data, but he was no expert. Gray picked up his phone, dialled the number listed in the email footer.

"Dr Aplin? Solomon Gray of Thanet CID. Have you got a few minutes to discuss the results you sent through?"

"Absolutely, and its Amy. What do you want to know?" Her accent was soft Welsh.

"I could do with a brief summary, to be honest."

"How far did you get into my report?"

"Page two, sorry."

Aplin laughed. "At least you're honest."

"It happens occasionally."

She chuckled again. "Well, first and foremost, the two subjects aren't related. If you go to the opening page of the report, you'll see several graphs, each with vertical bars of varying height."

He scrolled up. "Got them."

"Fundamentally, the information is stored as a digital code, based on the nomenclature of what are called Short Term Random Repeats. This is a microsatellite consisting of a unit of between two and thirteen nucleotides repeated a multiple

"

of times along the row of a DNA strand. What we do in the STR analysis is count the exact number of repeating units. The number of times these units occur can be highly variable between people. Does that make sense?"

"Well enough for me to follow."

"So, back to the graphs. One plot is from the baby, the other Polly Draper. What you can see is a clear difference in the repetition of the STRs. I'd say there's less than a 1% chance of a family connection between the subjects."

"That's certainly definitive."

"There's a further aspect you may have missed. If you flip on, you'll see the chart for Philip Ogilvy. Have you got it?"

Gray did so. "Yes."

"Okay, compare Polly Draper's graph to Philip Ogilvy's." Gray did, flipping back and forth several times.

"They appear different. The lines don't overlap as much."

"Absolutely. So, the siblings have a match with their mother, but I would suggest they have different fathers."

"Ouch."

"I thought I should bring it to your attention, in case it's pertinent to the case."

Gray sat back and thought. "At this stage that's impossible to say, Amy."

"What will you do?"

"I need to consider the options. Thanks for your help."

"Don't be so quick to get off the phone. There's more. I've just had the results of the familial search. We had several cold hits."

"You came up with names?"

"A few. Seventeen possibilities in total."

"Bloody hell, that'll take some checking out." Gray imagined all the leg work involved in tracking down each relative, visiting them, taking statements and gaining their consent for a swab to then cross-reference against their data. He'd known familial analyses would throw up several comparisons, but he'd hoped for a smaller number. Hamson would not be pleased based on their recent discussion.

"I've a suggestion which may help you. I can run the DNA through a commercial database and see if that throws anything up."

"Commercial database?"

"The ones that are always being advertised on TV. Where you buy a kit, send your DNA off to them and they come back with your genealogy."

"I don't know why anyone would do that."

"Plenty of people have. The commercial databases evaluate single nucleotide polymorphisms. They possess 600,000 to 700,000 connections so these are far more detailed than the STRs, sufficient to detect even distant family ties. The databases have been used in the US to clear up several cold cases where unwitting relatives sent in swabs and a family connection was subsequently made."

"What's the downside?"

"At worst it won't bring down the target list from 17 and there's a cost associated."

"So, our position could remain neutral, but our budget gets hit with another bill."

"Yes, but I'd be surprised if some benefit wasn't seen. It could bring the list down to a handful of priority targets."

"How long will it take?"

"I can probably get you an answer tomorrow."

Pfeffer glanced into his office then started to walk away. Gray covered up the mouthpiece, called, "I'm almost finished, Melanie. Come in." Pfeffer did so and leant against the wall.

"Do it," said Gray. "And thanks for your help."

"I'll be back in touch soon as I can." Aplin rang off.

Gray replaced the receiver, said to Pfeffer, "That was the labs; they're going to carry out some further tests, hopefully to reduce the targets from the familial search."

"Good because I was going to ask you how we should proceed from here."

"For now, hold off. We can reassess tomorrow."

"You saw that the children are only half related?"

"Yes, sticky one that."

"Are you planning on telling them?"

"It's not really our place, is it?"

"Don't they deserve to know?"

"Would you want to if it was you?"

"Yes. And what if it has a bearing? Like if Andrea had an affair and it was covered up?"

Gray sat back. "Draper is 27 and Ogilvy 36, the baby died no more than a decade ago, when Andrea was approximately 68. I can't see how it fits."

"You're the boss," said Pfeffer. "But I think you're wrong to say nothing." She pushed off the wall and left.

Gray dialled Draper's number.

Thirteen

Polly Draper lived only a few streets away from her mother's house on Harrow Dene, a large estate of much newer properties maybe 40 or 50 years old. Hers was a chalet-style detached house with a steeply pitched roof partly hidden behind a high perennial hedge.

Gray knocked on the door. Immediately there was barking from inside, then a small shape jumping up at the frosted glass door. A larger shadow appeared shortly after. Draper opened up, bent over, holding onto Mack's collar. "Inspector Gray, come in."

"Thanks, I won't keep you long." Draper closed the door and let go of the dog. Mack leapt at Gray, tongue out and seemingly happy to see him.

"Mack, get down!" Mack backed up. "Sorry about that."

"He's okay." Gray squatted, put his hand out. Mack gleefully accepted a stroke. "You took him then?"

"I had to." Mack rolled over onto his back, paws in the air, exposing his stomach. Gray rubbed the dog's ribs. "It's only temporary. Until I can find somewhere permanent. The kids love him but he's driving my husband up the wall."

Gray gave Mack one more rub, then stood, said, "I've got an update for you."

"Okay, come through." Draper indicated the living room. A huge television dominated one wall in front of which was arranged a leather sofa and armchairs, like an upmarket cinema. "Please, take a seat." Mack followed them, waited to see where Gray was going to sit, then flopped at his feet.

The leather squeaked as Gray settled into the armchair. "We've carried out some tests on the baby." He didn't want to say post-mortem. Sometimes people were squeamish about the process and didn't like to think directly about it. "First, you were right, it was a girl."

Draper frowned. "So sad."

"Second, we've received the DNA analysis back from your swabs and we found that the girl is not related to you or your mother."

"Oh!" Draper put a hand over her mouth. "I'm not sure whether that's a relief or not." She shook her head. "How did she die?"

"Most probably of natural causes and no more than ten years ago but at the moment it's difficult to be more specific."

"She lay there for a decade?"

"So it seems."

"That's horrible. How did she end up in my mother's wardrobe?"

"I don't know yet."

"But you'll tell me when you do?"

"Of course."

"What happens to the little girl now?"

"We'll keep her for the time being."

"She'll be buried eventually, though?"

"Once our investigations are complete. At the moment we're not clear who we should release her body to."

"God, of course. I never even thought about that."

"She's being treated with complete respect."

"It's about time someone did."

Gray agreed. "How are you otherwise?"

"Not enjoying being a minor celebrity, I have to say. I'm sure you've seen the newspapers?"

"Yes."

"There's been a couple of calls from reporters too. I've declined to comment."

"Probably for the best." Gray stood, Mack lifted his head. "I'd better be on my way."

"Was that all you found from the swabs?" Draper remained seated. "About my relationship with the baby?"

"What do you mean?"

"You didn't make mention of Philip."

Gray groaned inside. He sat. "I was talking in general terms."

"You don't need to hide anything. I do know about my partial relationship to Philip."

"I wasn't sure how to broach it."

"I don't blame you. Clearly Mum was an expert at keeping secrets. She told me a few years ago that Philip and I were half-brother and sister."

"Philip isn't aware?"

Draper shook her head. "As you probably noticed he's a gloomy person. She didn't want to make it worse for him, she said. But I've never been sure whether to believe her. Even more so after discovering the baby. That made me question everything, to be honest."

Gray sat back down. "The DNA analysis revealed only a 50% match between you and Philip. You've got different fathers."

"So, at least that was true."

"I'm sorry."

"What are you apologising for?"

"I've no idea."

"Mum didn't have an affair, by the way."

"It's really none of my business."

"I can't let you leave with only half that story too. Mum was already pregnant when she and Dad got together. They'd known each other for years. Dad had loved Mum all that time but not been able to do anything about it because she had a boyfriend. But when her partner learned she was pregnant he ran away, leaving Mum in the lurch."

"Nice guy."

"Mum's parents were strict so there would have been a lot of shame heaped on her if she'd borne a child out of wedlock. So, in stepped my father. They married quickly and he took Philip as his own son."

"Sounds like he was a good man."

"Thank you. He was. I miss him a lot. Mum told me all this just after Dad died, then swore me to secrecy."

"And it'll stay that way."

"I appreciate it." Draper smiled. "Now you can go." Mack followed them to the door. "Are you sure you can't take him?"

"Sorry." Gray gave Mack one last rub before he left.

In his car Gray sat, considering what Draper had told him. Family secrets and sources of shame. He wondered if the mother of the baby in the box had felt the same. Had shame driven her to act?

Gray's phone rang.

"Doctor Maltby from the QEQM. Somebody has just walked into A&E with dog bites."

Fourteen

The Spencer Wing parking spaces were all filled so Gray had to pay at a machine. He marched inside the hospital, ignoring the triage line run by the nurse, a different one to last time, and went up to the desk. He showed his warrant card to the receptionist. "Doctor Maltby is expecting me," he said.

She picked up her phone, dialled, waited a moment for an answer, said, "The police officer is here." She listened, replaced the receiver. "Doctor Maltby will let you in."

"Thanks."

Gray moved to the double doors which led to the A&E suite. A moment later the door opened, Maltby standing there in her white lab coat. "That was fast." She stood back, allowed Gray access.

"I was only down the road in St. Peter's."

"This way." Maltby led Gray to the beds in the narrow area of the main A&E section. She paused, spoke quietly. "All I know is he's called Eric. When he arrived, he'd been bitten and scratched by a dog. His father is with him too. We cleaned Eric up and gave him something for the pain."

Eric was in the bed furthest away. Maltby drew back the curtains. Gray stepped through and the doctor drew the curtains again. Eric lay propped up in bed. Both his arms were on top of the blanket and heavily bandaged. He looked to be in his mid-teens. His dark hair was a mess, scratches on his face and a swollen bottom lip.

A man sitting on a chair beside Eric stood. He was wearing a tracksuit, zipped up to the neck, tattoos on the back of both his hands. His hair was curly, his nose once broken and badly fixed. "Who are you?"

"Inspector Solomon Gray."

"Thought you was a cop. You need to find the bastard what did this to my kid."

"Which is why I'm here." Gray turned to the patient. "What happened, Eric?"

Eric focused on his father, seeking permission.

"Tell him, son. It's all right."

"I was minding my own business when out of nowhere some dog ran at me, knocked me off my bike, then started going for my arms."

"What type?"

"A cop dog."

"A German Shepherd?"

Eric shrugged. Gray pulled out his phone, entered a browser, pulled up a photo of the breed, showed the screen to Eric.

"That's the one."

"Where did this happen?"

"The Sunken Gardens."

A run-down relic of what had once been a grand formal layout of flowers and close-cropped lawns in the 1930s above the cliffs in the well-to-do area of Westbrook on the edge of Margate. The large grassed area was hidden in a deep dip behind flint walls, trees, shrubs and hedges. The houses overlooking the gardens were hundreds of yards away, the other direction was the cliff edge. A good location for trouble.

"How old are you?"

"Sixteen."

"And your surname, please."

Eric checked with his father again. Maybe it was ingrained into the kid never to tell the cops anything. Another nod.

"Abbott."

"What were you doing in the Gardens?"

"Waiting for my mates. They were late. When they arrived, the bloke ran off down towards the beach."

"Could you describe the man?"

"All I know is he was taller than me. He kept his face covered with a scarf and had his hood up."

"Why would he pick you?"

Eric shrugged. "No idea. I weren't up to nothing."

"Did he speak to you?"

"He told me I was trouble."

Abbott senior, who hadn't shared his name with Gray, cut in. "He doesn't know what trouble is yet. Look officer, why don't you get out there and find this guy rather than stand here with us?"

"Be assured we'll be looking into this as a matter of urgency. Have you got a number I can contact you on?" Abbott senior gave him a mobile number. "Thanks, I'll be in touch."

Gray raised a thumb at Eric and left the bedside. Abbott followed him. Gray paused. Doctor Maltby hung back. The man got up close to Gray. "If you don't track him down, I will, all right?"

"Leave it to us, sir."

"What would you do if it was your kid?"

Gray knew exactly but wasn't going to admit it. "As I said, we'll treat it with urgency."

"Another of his mates got attacked, it isn't right."

"Kirton, you mean?"

"No." Abbot's forehead creased. "He's fine."

"I interviewed him a couple of days ago. He'd been bitten by a dog too, over on the Newington Estate."

"Don't know what you're on about, mate. Alex is fine."

"Alex Kirton? Not Freddie?"

"Never heard of a Freddie Kirton."

"So, who's the third one? We don't have a name." Abbott eyed Gray with suspicion. "The more evidence we can gather the faster we'll be able to learn who did this."

"All right, Alfie Durrant."

"Thank you. That'll help me, I'm sure. I'll be in touch."

"Work fast, mate." Abbott glared at Gray briefly before turning and walking back to his son.

Maltby walked beside Gray, said, "He's intense."

"Somebody just assaulted his son; I can give him leeway on that."

Maltby pressed a button beside the door to let him out. "Good luck."

Fifteen

Gray entered Eric Abbott into the PNC search engine. Eric possessed an extensive record. Mainly low-level stuff like affray, criminal damage (graffiti which he'd claimed was street art and was given a warning) along with several anti-social behaviour orders. He was 16 and lived on Park Place, behind Dreamland in Margate. He'd attended the Hartsdown Academy junior school in the town until moving to the Marlowe Academy senior school at 14.

The list of known associates was relatively short – Alfie Durrant, Alex Kirton and Eric's father, Andrew Abbott. Gray jumped over to Abbott senior's record. Seemingly, the son was imitating the father because Abbott was a career criminal. He'd been inside for armed robbery as recently as four years ago. His place of residence was Westcliff Road, just a stone's throw from the Westbrook beach and near to the Sunken Gardens.

Next, Gray flipped over to Alfie Durrant. He was a little older than Eric at seventeen but had committed a raft of crimes of increasing severity, leading up to a house burglary a year ago for which he'd received six months in a juvenile detention centre.

Since his release there had been accusations of an assault on a pensioner in the College Square shopping centre, although the man refused to press charges and eventually the case had been dropped by the Crime Prosecution Service because they weren't convinced gaining a conviction was feasible – the man allegedly assaulted wasn't willing to testify.

Like Eric, Durrant was a Margate resident, living in one of the flats on Mill Lane, and had been at Hartsdown too before moving to the Marlowe. He'd left school at sixteen to attend the Broadstairs College but was now classified as unemployed having dropped out not even a year into the cookery course he'd begun.

Gray returned to Freddie Kirton. Freddie was younger at fifteen and unconnected to Abbott or Durrant other than being a Marlowe Academy pupil. It made sense why he would attend the school, his house was only a couple of streets away. Otherwise he lived in Ramsgate, the other side of the island, and had a minimal police record. So, the only link between all three was the school. And more than a thousand pupils attended the Marlowe from right across Thanet. Freddie was an outlier.

Then, Gray looked up Alex Kirton – the name Abbott had given him. The same age as Eric at 16, lived one street away, also attended Hartsdown and Marlowe, ran in the same gang as Eric and Durrant, and had even been picked up a couple of times accompanying Eric. Kirton too had avoided time in detention and had multiple ASBOs to his name. Gray looked up the arresting officer – PC Damian Boughton.

Which confirmed Freddie Kirton had to be mistaken identity and the games console with the apologetic note a way of making up for it. His attacker possessed a guilty conscience, it seemed.

So, three minors all with an ever-growing criminal record and, to all intents and purposes, that list would simply expand further as they moved into adulthood. Most of the crimes linked to the trio were in and around central Margate. Boughton's patch, hence the arrests. Gray called him.

"I'm on a day off, Sol," said Boughton when he answered.

"Sorry."

"It's all right, you weren't to know. To be honest I can do with the distraction; I'm only running a few errands for the wife. What's up?"

"It's who, not what."

"That makes no sense."

"Three males, Abbott, Kirton and Durrant. You've nicked all of them more than once in and around central Margate."

"Oh yes, I'm very familiar with that trio, real group of trouble causers. They used to be little bastards even when they were toddlers and are growing up to be big bastards as they reach adulthood. Between them and a couple of their mates they're responsible for the majority of the trouble in my patch. The only blessing is they're not involved with selling drugs, although that might just be a matter of time. They're a real worry for the future."

"Well, two of them have been assaulted in recent weeks, a man has set a dog on them."

Boughton laughed. "I didn't know that. Thoroughly deserved, I'd say."

"I'm trying to find out who attacked them."

"When you do, tell me would you? I'd like to shake them by the hand."

"Bloody hell, Damian."

"Look, Sol. You've read their records. Presumably you've also seen the laughable sentences the courts have handed down."

"They're minors."

"So? That makes it okay for them to harass and beat people up, break into their houses? Get drunk in public, make lewd suggestions to passers-by? Now is the time to come down hard on them, before it becomes totally ingrained, before they realise they can pretty much do as they please. You've experienced this behaviour; you can't tell me you haven't. And things will only get worse with the jails full to bursting, you watch."

"It's not our job to be the judge."

"They hardly even get in front of a judge, though. Mark my words, this lot will be in and out of our station over the next few years. Andrew Abbott is well connected. He used to work with one Frank McGavin." The self-exiled crime boss. "There's trouble ahead, for sure."

"Any idea who might target them?"

"I could give you a list as long as your arm! Besides their mothers nobody will care that they've been assaulted. Look, I've got to go."

"Wait, Damian."

"Okay but be quick."

"Didn't you want to talk to me about something?"

"I don't think so."

"You said the other day in St. Peter's."

"Oh, yes. It's nothing. Forget it. Anyway, I'd wish you good luck, but for once I hope you fail to catch your man. That lot deserve everything they get and more." Then Boughton was gone.

Gray sat back, vaguely dissatisfied with the conversation with Boughton. He scrolled through the Kirton's record one more time, not sure what he was looking for. He was about to exit when he noticed that someone else had recently accessed the file. Gray flipped to Durrant's and then to Eric. He saw the same name.

Jerry Worthington.

Sixteen

"Where's Worthington?" asked Gray.

"Are you alright, sir?" Ibbotson frowned.

"I'm after Worthington."

"Yes, sir. We're all aware of that." Ibbotson glanced around the office. Gray was aware of faces turned towards him.

"Jesus, Ted. Have you bloody seen him or not?"

"He's right behind you." Ibbotson nodded over Gray's shoulder.

Worthington stood with his arms crossed a few feet away near the door, wearing a mocking expression.

"My office," said Gray. "Now."

"Wasn't one bollocking enough?" asked Worthington. "What am I supposed to have done this time?"

"I'm here if you need me," said Ibbotson as Gray stalked away.

"Stay out of it, sergeant," said Gray over his shoulder.

Worthington entered the office first, Gray a couple of feet behind him. He slammed the door shut.

"What the hell is going on?" asked Worthington. "You're acting like someone has stolen your teddy bear."

"Eric Abbott, Alex Kirton and Alfie Durrant."

Worthington blinked, raised his hands out to the side. "Is that supposed to mean something?"

"Three lads in the same gang, two recently mauled by a dog with a third attacked in a case of mistaken identity."

"Sounds like pretty bad luck to me."

"What do you know about them?"

"I've no idea who you're talking about."

"Which is strange as you've accessed their records." Gray span around the computer screen, stabbed a finger at the line where the DC's name was listed along with a date and time.

"I'm telling you again, I don't know who they are."

"Yet your details are clearly detailed as having read the files."

"I can't explain that, other than to say it wasn't me!"

"I don't believe you!" Gray stepped closed to Worthington, fists clenched.

"I don't give a shit what you think!" Worthington squared up. He was a big guy, but Gray didn't care. "All you've ever done is hassle me since I started." Worthington got toe to toe with Gray.

"Bullshit! You're a liar, Worthington and as bent as they come!"

"I've never met those kids!"

"Who were you selling the information to this time?"

"Nobody!"

"You're dirty, Worthington."

Worthington's hand flashed out, grabbed Gray by the shirt, a fist raised ready to hit him.

"What the bloody hell is going on here?" Hamson stood in the doorway, Ibbotson at her shoulder. Beyond, the rest of the office watched open mouthed.

Worthington let go of Gray, stepped back. "Inspector Gray was pushing my buttons, ma'am."

"Not true," said Gray. "He's been selling information again."

"That's a lie!"

"Shut up, the both of you!" Hamson turned to Ibbotson, said, "Take Worthington to the canteen, buy him a coffee and calm him down."

"Ma'am."

Hamson stepped to one side, allowing Worthington to push past. "What are you lot looking at?" he snarled at the staring CID team.

"DC Worthington, don't make it any worse than it already is." He ignored Hamson. She turned to Gray. "My office, then you can explain what this debacle was about."

Gray trailed after Hamson, doing the walk of shame. Wyatt gave Gray a minor shake of the head, the disapproval clear. Pfeffer threw him an unconvincing smile. Hamson didn't speak to Gray until they were behind a closed door. "Go on, bullshit away."

"I've got the bastard."

"How? What, Sol? All I'm aware of is a slanging match between you and Worthington that resulted in Ibbotson calling me down and splitting the pair of you up."

"The boys who were attacked by the dog, Worthington accessed all their files."

"Okay."

"Several days *before* they were set upon."

"What's his explanation?"

"He doesn't have one, claims he's innocent, of course."

"Hang on. We have to be certain before accusing one of our own."

"We *know* Worthington is dirty."

"That was never proven, otherwise I'd have kicked him out myself."

"I'm positive."

"That's not enough. And this ... setting a dog onto kids, its extreme."

"Seemingly it's Worthington's way of putting a stop to their expanding life of crime."

"That's a very twisted logic."

"It's Worthington we're talking about here. We've got to deal with this. Kick him off the force, Von."

"You know I can't just do that. The best I can do is put this into the Professional Standards Department." They were a separate team who investigated complaints against the police. "See if he's got a case to answer."

"Surely we have adequate evidence to boot him out?"

"We have to go through the proper channels. If I just give Worthington the push without going through due process it'll probably end up in a tribunal with Worthington claiming I'm simply supporting a personal crusade by you."

"It bloody well is a crusade."

Hamson held up a hand. "All we have is an electronic access record. On its own I don't see that as sufficient. I'll take advice from HR as to whether I should suspend and refer him to the PSD. If they say yes, Worthington will be suspended, pending further investigation. If they say no, he stays."

"HR hasn't got the balls."

"Whatever, they're my final words on the matter."

"Seriously, Von…"

Hamson banged her palm on the desk. "Inspector Gray!" she shouted. "Stop! Gray held his hands up. "I think you need to go home for the day."

"You're kicking me out of the station and not Worthington?" Gray was incredulous.

"I'm shipping you both off. Obviously, neither of you are thinking straight. Take yourself home, clear your head, come back afresh tomorrow."

"What will the rest of the team think?"

"Seriously, Sol. When has that ever concerned you before? I'll speak with them." She pointed a finger. "Go."

Gray succeeded in not slamming Hamson's door. He paused in the connecting office, clenching and unclenching his fists before making his way to the stairs.

He rang Wyatt's mobile as he reached the car park. She answered. "Hang on." Gray heard the scrape of chair legs, then the squeak of hinges. "I'm in the corridor now. What's going on?"

"I'm being sent home, like a naughty schoolboy. Worthington too."

"By Hamson."

"That's right."

"Well done."

"Can you do me a favour?"

"Of course."

"Bring my laptop over when you leave?"

"Sure."

"I'll cook you dinner to say thank you."

"Do you have to, Sol? You're not the best chef."

"Kick a man when he's down."

"Look, I'd better go. I'm being told Hamson wants a quick word." Then she was gone.

Sixteen

The buzzer went earlier than Gray expected. He pressed the button to let Wyatt in, left the door on the latch. She'd been here plenty of times, knew her way around. He headed onto the balcony with two bottles of beer. He flipped the cap off of one, left the other for now. A couple of minutes later, Gray heard the lock click when Wyatt pushed the door to behind her.

"Hello, Sol." Pfeffer, not Wyatt, stood framed by the French window. She wore jeans and a white blouse, short hair slicked back.

"I thought you were Wyatt. She's bringing my laptop over."

"When?"

"If she's on time, less than half an hour."

"I won't be long. There's something I've got to tell you."

"Now?"

"Now. Otherwise, I might never say it."

"Fancy one?" Gray lifted the bottle.

"I'm not drinking at the moment." Pfeffer sat. "Things have been rather ... difficult since Wyatt came back to the station."

"For both of us."

"I'm pretty certain it's going to get worse soon."

"I don't understand, Melanie."

Pfeffer clasped her hands in her lap. "I'm pregnant."

Gray paused, the bottle halfway to his mouth. "What?"

"I'm expecting your baby."

"Are you sure?"

"One hundred per cent."

"How?"

"Do you want me to draw you a diagram? And before you ask, it's yours." Gray couldn't speak. "And I'm keeping it." A pause. "This is why I stopped fighting and cut out booze." A longer pause. "Say something, Sol."

"Christ."

"I'm sorry, I never meant for this to happen."

"You've nothing for which to apologise. When are you due?"

"July. And I'll be coming back to work after my maternity break."

"Well, we can figure all that out."

"I'm not expecting you to get involved, being a father, I mean. You don't need to come to the scans or the birth or anything like that."

"I want to." Though Gray wasn't sure at all what he was thinking right now.

"As you said, we can figure it out." Pfeffer stood. "Look, I'd better get going. Your girlfriend will be here soon."

Gray rose, made to kiss Pfeffer but she stepped back. "Sorry," he said.

"I'll let myself out." Pfeffer quietly closed the door behind her.

"Fucking hell." Gray drained the rest of his beer, opened the other. He was going to be a father again. Another thought occurred to him. He was going to have to tell Wyatt.

WYATT WAS A FEW MINUTES' late. "Sorry, I had to park further along the esplanade and walk back." She held out Gray's laptop.

Did he tell her now? If so, what should he say?

"Started already?" She meant the three empty beer bottles on the table, a fourth in Gray's hand.

"Sorry, bad day."

"I guess you won't want another one yet?"

"If you're going to the fridge I will."

Wyatt frowned but said nothing. When she came back, she put Gray's beer down on the table, said, "I can't see anything on the stove for dinner." She sat down.

"There's a lasagne in the fridge I'm going to microwave for us."

"As I thought, a culinary delight awaits."

"Sorry."

"Stop apologising."

"Sorry."

Wyatt rolled her eyes. They sat in silence for a few minutes. Gray wasn't sure where to begin. His instinct was to stay quiet. When this secret came out there was no putting it back.

"Hamson spoke with the CID team."

"Oh, yes, of course. How did it go?"

"I thought you'd be on at me as soon as I walked through the door to find out."

"I forgot." Wyatt blinked in surprise. "What did she say?"

"That you'd gone home with a stomach upset and to leave you alone."

"A stomach upset?"

"Nobody believed it. You were the talk of the station."

"Great." And he would be again once Pfeffer's news came out.

"Why don't I make us dinner?"

"If you want."

Gray carried on drinking, stared out to sea. Wyatt returned soon with two plates and a fork. She'd even managed to find some wilted salad from somewhere. Gray ate mechanically.

"What's going on, Sol?" asked Wyatt.

"Nothing, really."

"You're totally spaced out."

"Just tired. It's been a really strange day."

"All right, why don't I leave you alone?"

"If you want."

Wyatt's face fell. She clearly didn't want. Like Pfeffer, she shut the door quietly behind her.

Seventeen

Gray drove into work the following morning, his head still spinning. He'd drunk a lot more than he'd intended and barely slept, turning everything over in his mind. Several times Gray had picked up his mobile to call or message Pfeffer. On each occasion he'd held back.

His phone rang, intruding on his thoughts. "Good morning, Dr Aplin."

"Is now a good time?" she asked.

"Nothing's good at the moment."

"Sorry?"

"I'm in traffic so you'll help me not swear at other drivers." Gray pushed aside thoughts of Pfeffer.

Aplin laughed. "I've got feedback from the commercial laboratory regarding the cross-referenced DNA samples. It's good news. The list is down from seventeen to three."

"That's great, a much more manageable number."

"You'll have the information when you arrive at your desk."

"Thanks."

"No problem." Aplin rang off.

Gray missed a set of lights, arriving just as it turned red. He thumped the steering wheel in frustration.

GRAY WALKED THROUGH the Detective's Office, ignoring the glances from members of his team, curious still about his absence. Pfeffer wasn't in yet, or Worthington. Ibbotson kept his head down, like he hadn't noticed Gray.

"Morning, Ted," said Gray, simply to needle him.

"Oh, hi." Ibbotson flushed a bright red, cheering Gray up no end.

He kicked his office door shut, then fired up the computer. There, at the top of his email list, was the note from Aplin. In the note she gave a brief outline of her findings and the names as bullet points – Imogen Nicklin, Zara Jessop and Kerry Hudson.

The DNA reports for each prospect were attached too. Gray gave them a cursory glance, just to confirm the similarities were as Aplin stated. He moved to the PNC database to check for any records. Statistically, families stayed within the same local area. Meaning Gray would prioritise those within Thanet.

Immediately, Gray discounted Nicklin, a 33 year old Glaswegian and still resident there. She'd been arrested several times for selling Class A and Class B drugs as recently as six months ago and was on bail awaiting trial.

Next on the list was Jessop. She possessed an extensive record – and she was deceased. Eight years ago, cause of death was listed as accidental. Although she'd lived in Ramsgate her origin was the Medway town of Rochester.

Hudson, however, appeared far more interesting. She lived just a few miles away in Garlinge, a village off the Canterbury Road, roughly halfway between Margate and Birchington. She was 27 and had been arrested for criminal damage in her late teens. Her photo from then showed a surly Goth – long black hair, lots of black make-up and a sneer. She'd had no contact with the police since; perhaps her one blemish was a result of youthful angst. Gray wrote down her address too.

Gray switched his attention to the births, marriages and deaths database maintained by the British Government which recorded all of these events in the UK. Officially, two of the women hadn't registered a baby at all. The only parent was Nicklin with children delivered periodically over the last decade and to different fathers.

He picked up the notes. Hudson's address went into his pocket. He grabbed his jacket. Gray handed Ibbotson the paper with Nicklin's details on it. "Would you give Glasgow CID a call please and check into Imogen Nicklin. She's a possible relative to the baby in the box. I think it's unlikely, but I'd prefer to be certain there's no connection to Thanet." Ordinarily, he'd have asked Pfeffer but for obvious reasons he chose not to.

The sergeant took the note. "Of course, sir. I'll get onto it now."

"Morning, Em," said Gray.

Wyatt grinned. "Morning, yourself. Feeling better?"

"Sort of."

"No hangover?"

"Made of sterner stuff."

"I'm about to go and interview somebody and I suspect the discussion is going to be sensitive."

"So, you wanted somebody a touch more empathic than you?"

"Pretty much."

"What about Pfeffer?"

"I'd prefer you."

"I'm honoured." Wyatt sat back. "Before I agree, what's the problem?"

Gray perched on the edge of Wyatt's desk. "I'm about to ask someone if they hid a pregnancy."

"Okay, I can see why you'd need some female help with that. I'll get my coat, then you can bring me up to speed on the way to wherever we're going."

As Wyatt turned away Worthington entered the office. He paused, held the door for Pfeffer. Both of them ignored Gray.

DENT-DE-LION ROAD SAT towards the west of Garlinge and ran parallel with the Canterbury Road. Nearby was a medieval structure originally built by Sir Dent de Lion more than five hundred years ago to protect his estate from marauders. Only the gatehouse itself remained now, sandwiched between two far more modern properties.

The house Gray wanted was a small bungalow on the corner of a street called Noble Gardens opposite a large area of flat, open ground beyond which was the disused Manston airport. Gray stopped immediately outside the house, waited for Wyatt to join him at the gate. On the drive a black Audi was parked.

"Remember, Sol. If she gets difficult, let me take over," said Wyatt.

"I hadn't forgotten since you told me the last time." Which was two minutes ago. At the door Gray knocked. It was opened by a woman smartly dressed in a pinstripe trouser suit and high heels. It was hard to see a similarity between the file photo and her. Hudson had changed a lot in the intervening years, not least dropping the Goth image completely. Her eyes moved between Wyatt and Gray. "Yes?" Her tone was sharp, clipped, like she was busy.

"Inspector Gray, Thanet CID." He showed his warrant card. "And this is my colleague, Emily Wyatt. Are you Kerry Hudson?"

"Just for another couple of weeks until I get married."

"Congratulations."

"What's this about? I'm rather short on time." She flicked a glance at the watch on her wrist as emphasis.

"Maybe we should speak inside?"

Hudson stifled a sigh, opened the door wide to allow them entrance. "I've only got ten minutes before I need to be leaving. Got a house to show to clients." She shut the door but made no move out of the hallway.

"What do you do?"

"I work for a local estate agent's, Robson and Edwards. We're very busy these days, lots of interest in Margate particularly."

"Which I find puzzling."

"I could give you chapter and verse on the relative attractiveness of the town, but we've only nine minutes left now."

"We'll come to the point then," said Gray, producing a thin smile from Hudson. "Your name has come up in an investigation."

"Oh?" Hudson frowned. "That can't be right."

"You were arrested for criminal damage."

Hudson blinked. "That was years ago, and I haven't been in trouble again." Hudson waved away the issue. "Me and some friends broke into our local school. It was stupid, hanging around with older boys who used to lead me astray. I've grown up a lot since then and I'm sure it's not worth wasting your time over."

"I agree and we're not here about that. Your name came up in connection with another matter. You may have read about the baby in the box."

"Of course, who hasn't?"

"We're trying to trace the parents."

"And you think I may be able to tell you, what? Who the mother is?"

"Your DNA was a partial match to the baby."

"My DNA is still on file?"

"That's right. It was taken when you were arrested."

"I remember, but surely it would have been destroyed?"

"Clearly not."

"Look, what's going on here? I'm a respectable person with a good job, about to be married and you come here, to my house, making accusations that I'm the parent of a mummified baby!"

"Nobody is accusing you of anything, Miss Hudson."

"My name won't end up in the papers, will it?"

"Why would that happen?"

"I know what you police are like."

"Strictly only one of us is with the police, Miss Hudson," said Wyatt.

"And what do you do then?"

"I'm a liaison officer."

"I don't know what that means. I'm warning you; my future father-in-law is a lawyer. If anything about my past makes it into the papers or sullies my name at all we will be suing you and the authorities for a small fortune."

Hudson pushed her way past Gray, flung open the door. "Now, please leave."

"Miss Hudson."

"Go, I've nothing more to say."

Wyatt turned to Gray. "Do as Miss Hudson says."

"I'm not talking to you either," said Hudson to Wyatt.

"I suspect you've something to get off your chest. Better you tell me now than it come out later."

"You've no idea what you're talking about." But Hudson spoke quietly now.

Wyatt tilted her head. Gray went outside.

HE SAT IN THE CAR, watching the house. The minutes slowly rolled by until, eventually, the front door opened, and Wyatt stepped out alone. She closed the door behind herself and walked quickly over to the car.

"Well?" asked Gray.

"Just drive," said Wyatt.

"Where?"

"Anywhere, Sol. Then we'll talk."

Gray started the engine, pulled away, turned left a few hundred yards along and continued along a narrow road until it widened with enough space for a few cars to park just opposite the medieval gatehouse. Gray stopped. "All right?"

"I wanted us to be out of sight." Wyatt put her mobile down between them. "You need to hear this. I recorded what Hudson told me. To be honest it didn't take much pushing to reach this stage."

"Did she know you were taping her?"

"No comment." Wyatt tapped the screen.

"Start from the beginning, Kerry." Wyatt's voice sounded muffled over the phone's speaker.

"First name terms?" said Gray.

"Shhh, Sol."

"This is all off the record, right?" said Hudson. The tone in her voice said having this conversation was the last thing she wanted to do.

"Absolutely," said Wyatt.

"None of this can come out. If anybody asks, I'll deny everything. I'm not going to court. My fiancée doesn't know and I'm not screwing up my job, all right? I've worked bloody hard to get to where I am and put the past behind me."

"You have my word."

"What about him out there?" Hudson meant Gray.

"I can make him keep a secret."

There was a long moment of silence before Hudson said, "God, it was all such a long time ago." A pause. "I was just a child really."

"How old?" asked Wyatt.

"Seventeen. Legal, at least." Hudson gave a wry chuckle. "He was older than me, much older. But I suppose at that age, most men are."

"How did you meet?"

"He was friends with my foster parents. I'd seen him around since I moved in with them."

"When was this?"

"Just after my 15th birthday. So, he was a familiar, kind face."

"How did your relationship start?"

"It's hard to be specific, really. It just sort of ... developed. I was growing up, becoming more independent, like you do when you're in Sixth Form. I went out for a drink with some friends from school and he was in the pub. We just got chatting. He asked if I came here often." Hudson laughed. "That old cheesy line. He bought me a few more drinks, soon my friends left, and it was just me and him.

"We arranged to meet again which we did, several times. I felt very mature, going out on dates. They were always scooting off to out of the way places, like Reculver. He'd pick me up in his car around the corner from where I lived. Eventually we fell into bed. It didn't feel like he groomed me or anything like that. I was almost an adult. Looking back now I still feel everything was totally consensual."

"How long were you in a relationship with this man?"

"A few months. Until I fell pregnant." A pause. "Which is when it got nasty."

"What happened?"

"He threatened me. I'd won a place at University on a grant. He told me to get rid of the child or I'd lose the money."

"Could he do that?"

"I don't know, it certainly felt that way by how he spoke. I wasn't going to keep the kid anyway, there was no way I could study with a baby, could I?"

"So, you had the termination?"

"Yes, and I've never thought about it since. It was the right thing to do."

"I went off to Bristol, came back a few years ago, met Jake and I'll become his wife soon. We can have our own children. Things are great and I don't want to mess them up because of a stupid mistake from years ago."

"What about the man who got you pregnant?"

"He never contacted me again and I haven't seen him either."

"Can you tell me his name?"

"No, never."

"Why?"

"He still lives in the area. I'm really not getting into all of that."

"We will be totally confidential."

"I've told you all I'm willing to. Nothing illegal went on. It's time for you to leave now too."

Wyatt leant over, stopped the playback. "And after that I was out on the street. When she makes her mind up, she sticks to it."

"So I found," said Gray. "She's 27 so all this would be nine or ten years back."

"That's right."

"Too early for the baby in the box to be hers."

"She had a termination, Sol. There was no baby."

"Assuming she told the truth.

"I believe her."

"All right, then she's not the mother we want."

"No."

"Did you get any indication at all who this man might be?"

"You heard what she said, Sol."

"The fostering connection was interesting. That guy you passed on the details of, Vardie, I've met him. I'll ask him to access the records and maybe we can speak to the people. I'll call him."

Gray got Vardie's voicemail, as usual. "Inspector Gray here, I'm trying to reach you with a couple of questions. I'll send you an email with them but please call me when you've had chance to take a look." He disconnected. "I didn't realise social services were so busy."

"We live in a generally sad world, Sol," said Wyatt.

"Very heartening."

Gray performed a U-turn. When they passed Hudson's house her car was gone. They were back on the Canterbury Road when his mobile rang. Vardie's voice came over the speakers. "Sorry I missed your call, Inspector."

"I've got a couple of questions for you."

"Well, I'm in the office, why don't you pop in when you're passing by?"

Eighteen

This time Gray parked around the rear of the social services building. The same Asian receptionist was on the desk. Vardie didn't make them wait long. When he came down the stairs, he was wearing a bottle green three-piece suit.

"Good to see you again," said Vardie.

"Emily Wyatt." She handed her card over.

Vardie read it with interest. "CEOP? Not after my job, Mrs Wyatt?"

Wyatt laughed, said, "It's Miss and I'm temporarily assigned to Thanet Police."

"Come on up." Vardie led the way. "Do you want a drink? It's just a machine, I'm afraid."

"We won't be keeping you long," said Gray.

"Probably for the best. The vegetable soup is particularly vile."

They went into the meeting room again. Vardie's laptop was sitting on the work surface. He pulled out a chair for Wyatt, leaving Gray to fend for himself. Wyatt winked at Gray as he sat.

"Now, you mentioned more questions? I assume they're related to your baby case?"

"Three names have come up – Imogen Nicklin, Kerry Hudson and Zara Jessop."

"Who do you want to start with?" Vardie pulled the laptop over, tapped in his password.

"Might as well go from the top."

"Imogen Nicklin then." More tapping, a pause. "We don't have any information on Nicklin. If she ever lived in Thanet, there was no involvement with Social Services. Next, Kerry Hudson you said?"

"That's right."

"I play lots of memory games." Vardie tapped the tip of a finger against his temple. A brief pause. "Okay, according to the files she was a local girl essentially born into fostering. Hudson was immediately removed from her mother; she didn't even get chance to take her home from the hospital. The father isn't known. Hudson then moved around between a number of carers in her earliest years before settling in one place when she was seven where Hudson stayed all the way through until she was eighteen."

"Any details of her having a child?"

"Not in the time we have records for."

"Then we come onto Zara Jessop. She was homeless, living on the streets. She spent a night or two at a hostel near your station, The Lighthouse." Gray knew the location, just behind the Dreamland amusement arcade off the seafront. "But its mainly men staying there, and it wasn't ideal for a young girl. So, the manager, Natalie Peace, got in touch with us and we found Miss Jessop a short-term foster." Vardie frowned. "Hmm that's interesting."

"What?"

"Both girls stayed with Andrea Ogilvy."

Gray glanced at Wyatt, said, "Is that unusual?"

"Not particularly. As we discussed when we first met, Andrea was one of our go-to carers in times of need. And Miss Jessop was definitely in need."

"How long did she stay with Andrea?"

"The first time was for a couple of months."

"She was there more than once?"

"That's right. More than a year between her stays. On the second occasion she was with Andrea for longer until she was just over 17. She moved into a council flat in Ramsgate. After that, we lost touch with her. And there's no indication Jessop had a child either."

"And there would have been an overlap between Hudson and Jessop staying with Andrea?"

"The first time yes, the second, no. Hudson had relocated. That's pretty much all I can tell you."

"Very helpful, Mr Vardie."

"Get in touch again if I can help with anything else." When they were downstairs Vardie handed his card to Wyatt. "As you don't have my details." He smiled.

When they sat in the car Gray stated the obvious. "Jessop and Hudson knew each other, and they were both with Andrea."

"Does it mean something?"

"I've no idea." Gray started the engine. "What did you think to Vardie?"

"Nice."

"Really?"

"Why, jealous?"

Gray snorted.

Nineteen

Gray turned his attention to the next most likely person on the DNA list – Zara Jessop. He pulled her police files again to go over in more detail.

Eight years ago she'd died; cause of death was listed as accidental. And Jessop was not even 18 when she passed. She'd been arrested multiple times for soliciting sex and possession of Class A drugs. Her hometown was Rochester, one of the Medway towns about forty-five miles and an hour's drive away. Her mug shot, taken months before she died, revealed a sad, angry girl who appeared much younger than her years – perhaps that was her unique selling point. Unkempt hair, gaudy lipstick and grinning as if she was high.

She'd lived at a flat in Ramsgate on Albert Street on the corner of Grundy's Hill, just a few roads back from the Royal Harbour. Gray knew the place, a low-rent block housing mainly people on benefits. Her place of work was Platinum, a lap dancing club over in Ramsgate.

Next, Gray moved to the crime scene report. *"Jesus."* He recognised the name of the senior investigating officer. Detective Sergeant Mike Fowler.

They'd been close friends. Fowler too was deceased; Gray had seen him die. Anything involving Fowler immediately raised concern in Gray's mind. He'd been a good cop, though with some bad leanings. Could he have tainted the investigation? For now, Gray needed to push that particular thought to one side.

Jessop's body had been discovered in her flat after a concerned friend phoned the police, worried she hadn't been seen for a few days and the flat was locked up tight.

Two uniformed officers forced their way in, breaking the Yale latch on the front door, finding Jessop stretched out on her back on the living room floor. There were no signs of forced entry – all the windows were closed despite it being a warm summer. The crime scene report focused on two aspects: an open bottle of alcohol beside the body, which had drained its contents into the carpet; and evidence of blood and bone matter on the wooden fire surround above the body. The friend was named as Lucy Gold, a co-worker of Jessop's at Platinum.

Gray moved to the post-mortem report. Actually, there were two, carried out several days apart. Clough, as the forensic pathologist who'd attended the scene, performed the initial PM. The follow up PM was undertaken by Amos Jenkinson. At the time Jenkinson would have been Clough's superior. Again, Gray scanned through the documents. Their conclusions were very similar.

The level of hypostatis indicated the body had remained in the position in which she'd died. Several photos of the corpse showed large purple livid patches on her back, caused by the settling of the blood because the heart no longer pumped the fluid around the body. Once the heart stopped gravity took hold and the blood drained to the lowest point. If the body had been repositioned following death then a shadowing would often be seen as the blood moved again, forming a second set of patterns. But there was no shadow, so she'd remained in this one position.

Cause of death was concluded as a single injury to the rear of the skull, caused by blunt force trauma. The shape of the wound, long, narrow and wedge-shaped, matched that of the fire surround. Photographs from the scene and the skull concurred. Clough's notes revealed several marks along the forearm from needles –they were old.

Along with the PM data was a toxicity report. Jessop's bodily fluids had been tested. No drugs, so she was no longer a user, but there was a high level of alcohol present, enough to have put her more than three times over the drink driving limit. Jessop was relatively small – just over five feet and weighed only 57 kilos – here Gray had to convert to the imperial measurement – slightly under 9 stones.

Finally, Gray flipped to the inquest into her death. It was Jenkinson, not Clough, who'd attended. The details were brief as the hearing was short. The evidence all pointed towards accidental death. The conclusion was that Jessop had been highly inebriated, fell backwards and banged her head. Death would have been almost immediate.

Gray read over everything again. Slower this time, in case he'd missed anything. No mention of a recent pregnancy. Neither Clough's nor Jenkinson's PM report stated as such. So, she didn't appear to be the mother, either.

Ibbotson knocked on Gray's door. "Sir," he said, "Glasgow CID have been back on. They've visited Imogen Nicklin. She claims to never even have heard of Thanet, never mind visited here."

"That's a pretty definitive no, then."

"I'd say so. Thanks Ted." Ibbotson left.

Gray picked up the phone and called Dr Aplin. When she answered he said, "I've got a quick question for you. If none of the three women your analysis has targeted is the mother, what would be our next steps?"

"You'll just have to wait for more DNA. There will probably be additional hits in the future."

"That's it?"

"Pretty much, we can only test against the samples that we have, I'm afraid. The NDNAD database is the biggest in the world. We find a match against a suspect in about 60% of cases. About 80% are men and mainly Northern European. As we discussed, the commercial databases are a rich source of information but not everybody's details are available. Sorry I can't be more helpful."

"That's fine, thanks for letting me know." Gray disconnected.

Gray had a contact number from the records for Zara's mother. Her first name was Susan. He picked up the phone and tapped in the number. It was answered after a couple of rings. "Hello, Jessop residence."

"Am I speaking with Mrs Jessop?"

"I rather thought that would be obvious." She sounded well educated, her accent bordering on upper class, southern and privileged. Like BBC newsreaders from fifty years ago.

"My name is Detective Inspector Solomon Gray, I'm with the Thanet police."

A deep intake of breath came down the line. "Would this be to do with Zara?"

"It is."

"Then you're wasting your time, Inspector, I'm done discussing her." Her tone was haughty and dismissive, immediately getting Gray's back up.

"I have some questions I want to ask."

"I'm afraid that's impossible."

"They're to do with your daughter's death."

"I don't want to think about her. It was a long time ago."

"Her name was Zara." Mrs Jessop snorted in response. Gray continued, "My questions are important. When we're finished you won't hear from me again."

"Frankly, I don't want to hear from you now, inspector."

"Mrs Jessop, somehow, some way, we will be talking." In reality, Gray couldn't force Jessop to comply.

A long silence which Gray didn't fill then a sigh. "If you insist. I've a few minutes."

"I want to see you face to face."

"At my house?"

"Yes, Mrs Jessop."

"You're a nasty man."

"I assume that's a yes?"

"It is. When will you arrive?"

"Within the hour."

"I expect you not to overstay your welcome."

She disconnected, robbing Gray of the opportunity to state he had absolutely no intention of spending any longer with her than he had to.

Twenty

Gray barely knew Rochester. He'd been there once to walk the historic heart when his kids were small. He remembered there was a castle built by William the Conqueror and that Charles Dickens had spent a lot of time in the town – the famous writer once had a country home the other side of the river. In fact, Dickens had died there.

He followed the sat nav's command and took the junction off the M2, the motorway connecting Thanet to London. He followed the A229, a wide road with houses and grass verges either side, trees dotted periodically, straight north for several miles.

As he neared the centre of town the traffic flow congealed to a crawl and the buildings crowded together. Eventually the sat nav instructed him to head east – Susan Jessop lived not far from the river. His progress slowed to a crawl with bumper to bumper vehicle queues. When Gray finally arrived, he realised the road was narrow and parking was impossible – double yellow lines prevented anyone stopping. Even leaving a motorbike here would block the route.

Gray drove around the immediate area for a few minutes before he managed to find a space a few streets away in a time restricted zone. He had an hour. As he got out of his car, he caught the eye of a traffic warden in a blue uniform and peaked cap a few yards away writing in his notebook. He'd be making a list of registration numbers. The warden would return in precisely sixty minutes to catch anyone who'd overstayed. They operated on a basic wage and commission – cash for each driver they hit with a fine. Gray checked the time and got walking.

He wouldn't be lining anybody's pocket.

THE JESSOP RESIDENCE was set back behind a low wall, topped with an ornate, painted metal fence. The small garden was neat, the bushes cut back ready for spring. The house itself was arranged over three stories, dark red brick, white painted sash windows, maybe Georgian architecture, definitely old. Gray couldn't see inside because nets hung at the windows. He lifted a heavy cast iron knocker and rapped on the door. It was opened by a dapper lady in her 50s.

"Inspector Gray, you're late."

"There's nowhere to park nearby."

"It's the middle of the day." She stepped back. "Get yourself in."

The hallway was well lit. Stairs led upwards just in front. The walls were decorated with a floral green paper, the floor stripped, and boards varnished. Standing by the bannister was a young man. He had the same aquiline nose as Mrs Jessop and was dressed in a black suit and bright red tie.

"My son, Edgar" said Mrs Jessop, "He's a lawyer."

"Pleased to meet you," said Edgar. "And I'm not yet fully qualified."

Mrs Jessop glared at her son. She'd wanted to establish that she had legal representation to hand.

"Take them off," she pointed to Gray's shoes. "Put them there with the rest, next to Edgar."

Gray shucked his shoes, not bothering to undo the laces. "Fortunately, I've got my good socks on today."

Mrs Jessop huffed while Edgar coughed in an attempt to suppress a chuckle. A disapproving Mrs Jessop led Gray and Edgar through the first doorway. A big open fireplace was set in one wall. The floor was the same varnished boards as the hallway, but a rug filled most of the space. The furniture looked heavy. Thick curtains either side of the windows. The light was dim because of the nets.

She pointed to a high back chair and took one herself. Edgar perched nearby on a stool. The space looked and smelled like a rarely used reception room.

She sat back, crossed her legs at the ankle and folded her fingers in her lap. "Well, Inspector Gray, you mentioned something involving my daughter?" Her tone was cool. "She's passed, you know. I hardly see her causing any more trouble now, do you?"

"I'm working on a case in which your daughter had some form an involvement."

"Case? What case?"

"I'm not at liberty to say. What can you tell me about her?"

Jessop sighed. "Where to start? She was brought up correctly. As you can see, we come from a reasonable background. She could have had whatever she wanted, really. But what we offered wasn't suitable. She started to get into trouble at school. We were paying a lot of money for her education, I'll tell you. Eventually she got herself expelled."

"Why?"

"Boys, drink, drugs. It was shameful." Gray noticed Edgar pulling a face. Mrs Jessop continued, "She ran away when she was fourteen. We found her, in London on the streets, and brought her back. She left again at fifteen, twice. London again, then Thanet. When she reached sixteen and disappeared the next time, we let go of her. She clearly didn't want to be with us."

"Do you know where she went?"

"Thanet, but not until the police contacted us after her death. That's when we found out."

"And you didn't have any contact with her in between?"

"As I said, Zara clearly didn't wish to."

"Why?"

Mrs Jessop leaned forward. "Do you have children, Inspector Gray?"

"Yes."

"Did they ever stop talking to you?"

"When they were teenagers."

"What about now?"

"Our relationship is decent enough."

"Then you're lucky." Mrs Jessop sat back again, regaining her seemingly relaxed posture. "Zara and I fought all the time. It felt like from the moment we met we didn't get on."

"Met?" It was a strange word to use.

"I was step-mother to Zara. Edgar is her half-brother."

"What about your husband? Did he try to speak with her?"

"Charles was in complete agreement with me throughout." It sounded like there was no room for argument between husband and wife. "And we weren't aware of any of her doings while she lived in Margate."

"There's nothing you can tell me at all?"

"No." She checked her watch. "Now, I'd better be getting on."

"That's it?"

"I informed you of two things. One I could only give you a few minutes. And two, you were wasting your time driving here, Inspector Gray. Unsurprisingly I was proven correct on both counts." She turned to Edgar and nodded.

"I'll show you out," said Edgar. He opened the front door for Gray to step through. Gray turned, expecting to say goodbye, but Edgar exited also. He pulled the door closed behind him. "She's at the window, watching, come on." Edgar led Gray onto the pavement. He pointed along the street. "So, she thinks I'm giving you directions."

"What's going on?" Gray couldn't withdraw, Edgar still had held his arm.

"Mother was wrong about Zara. Mother drove her away with her incessant nagging though she'll never admit it." Gray opened his mouth to ask another question, Edgar stopped him. "If I stay any longer, she'll be suspicious. Here, take these." Edgar withdrew some envelopes, tied together with string from an inside pocket and passed them to Gray. "Don't let her see these." Gray slid them into his jacket and Edgar retreated. The whole process had been hidden by their proximity. "My number is on a card inside one of them, if you want to speak."

Then Edgar turned away and headed back to the house. Mrs Jessop was at the window, the net lifted. She kept her eyes on Gray until he walked round the corner and out of sight.

GRAY SAT IN HIS CAR and pulled the package Edgar had given him from out of his pocket. He undid the knot and fanned out the envelopes. There were five in total, the postmarks from Ramsgate and Margate, and from approximately eight to ten years ago. He flipped the uppermost envelope over. It had been neatly slit at the top, like Edgar had used a knife.

The letter inside was on a single sheet. The handwriting was shaky and sloped downwards. The layout was textbook, Zara's address top right, which he recognised from the PNC search, the date, then lower on the left was Edgar's address.

Dear Edgar,

I hope you're well. I wish I could see you. Is your mother still being a bitch? I'm sorry, I can't think of her as anything other than that after the way she's treated me.

I have some good news, I'm to be a mother myself! I've known for a while but didn't want to tell anyone in case I jinxed it. I'm sure I'm having a boy, he's very active. I've had to stop work as my stomach has become obvious. Nobody wants to pay to watch a pregnant dancer – except the occasional weirdo, and I'm not into that stuff...

I've told the father, he's ecstatic, but worried because he's already married. I know, I know, I'm a home breaker, however he's been really unhappy in his marriage for years. She's not his type and never has been. He's already got children, they're all grown up, so I'm sure we will have a lot of support. I'd really like you to meet him, and the baby once he's arrived. Do you think you can get away from The Witch for a few days? Ramsgate isn't that far away from Rochester!

Anyway, I must dash. Speak soon.

All my love.

Z x

Gray blinked, went back to the date again, it wasn't long before Zara's suicide. She'd mentioned a baby. She must have given birth in between then and her death.

Perhaps Zara was the mother of the baby in the box? Yet Clough and Jenkinson said nothing about any signs of pregnancy in their PM reports. Unless she'd lost the child?

Someone knocked on his window. The traffic warden. He tapped on his watch, indicating Gray's time was up. Gray showed the man his warrant card. The warden shrugged, a half sneer on his face, and hiked a thumb for Gray to move on. Gray put the letters on the passenger seat, started the engine and pulled away.

GRAY MOVED A FEW STREETS away and found a spot in a car park. The space was allocated to the disabled and the car park pay and display, but he didn't need long and he couldn't drive back to Thanet before reading further.

He sorted the letters into date order. The earliest was when Zara had run away to London. Living on the streets, she said. The picture she painted was grim and depressing. Of the near-impossible task of trying to find a hostel bed for the night and, if not there, then somewhere safe and warm. A public toilet, the kind you had to pay to get into, seemed the best. Sleeping in a place like that, though. Gray shuddered.

There was worse. Some guy had attempted to rape her. A fifteen-year-old. The short paragraph had been dismissive, as if it was just one of those things.

The subsequent three letters were about Zara moving to Thanet around a year later. Finding somewhere to live and then getting a job. She named the club – Platinum, a back-street joint in Ramsgate.

And she again mentioned meeting someone, who took pity on her and would look after her. An unnamed professional, white collar worker in a responsible job. Zara's benefactor was older, clearly (but at her age that could encompass a lot of people). And no mention of where or how they met.

Gray pulled out Edgar's card and dialled the number.

"Hello?" Edgar answered, sounding uncertain, street noise in the background.

"Thanks for the letters," said Gray.

"Were they helpful?"

"More than you could believe."

"Good, that's a relief. When I heard you were coming, I insisted I be there. It was father who went to London and brought Zara back, you know."

"That was a good thing to do."

"But it was all for nothing."

Gray had no answer to that. "Do you know what happened to her baby?"

"We talked on the phone just before she died. She said she was going to give it up for adoption, because she was struggling to cope. I never knew any more after that."

"And did Zara ever say who the father was?"

"No. But I'm convinced he had something to do with her death, Inspector."

"Based on what?"

"Instinct."

"I need more than that," said Gray. "Why were you suspicious of the father?"

Edgar paused while he thought. "I don't know, inspector. It was just a feeling I had. I couldn't put my finger on it then, either. He just didn't feel right. I can't tell you anymore, I'm sorry." Edgar rang off.

Gray felt vaguely unsatisfied. That he'd taken one further small step in the shadows but still didn't have a clear picture of events. Most of the people who'd been directly involved in events eight years ago – Jessop, Fowler, Jenkinson, Ogilvy – were either dead or incapable. But there was one who may be able to tell him more.

"Sol, you must be a mind reader," said Clough, the pathologist. "I've had the test results on the baby girl. They all came back negative. Therefore, I'm recording cause of death as Sudden Infant Death Syndrome. Just one of those sad, unexplained events."

"Good to know, but that wasn't the reason I rang."

"Sounds mysterious."

"Zara Jessop."

Clough's intake of breath was obvious over the phone. "What do you want to know?"

Twenty One

"I would have happily come over to Canterbury," said Gray as he sat down with a pint and an apple juice.

"I prefer to keep a separation between where I live and work," said Clough. "When I go home, I leave everything at the office. Besides, I wanted to speak as soon as possible. I've been on tenterhooks ever since you rang."

Gray had driven straight here from Rochester. They were meeting in the Belle Vue Tavern, a deceptively large pub on a narrow road on the very edge of Ramsgate. The cliff-top beer garden overlooked the huge expanse of Pegwell Bay and across to the old pharmaceutical site near Sandwich where thousands had once worked until the company shut its doors and moved. On a clear day the pier in Deal, where Wyatt lived, could be seen as a small strip jutting out into the English Channel.

Clough had picked a table around the corner from the bar, tucked away. As it was still relatively early, not quite 6pm, the place was relatively empty. Soon it would fill with people here to eat.

"By your reaction you clearly remembered Zara," said Gray.

"First, tell me why she's come up."

"She's possibly the mother of the baby in the box."

"Fuck." Clough removed his glasses, dropped them on the table, squeezed his eyes shut. Gray didn't think he'd ever heard Clough swear before. He allowed the silence to stretch until eventually Clough focused on Gray again. The pathologist's eyes were bloodshot. "I'll never forget her. She was the first PM I conducted on my own here and it created merry hell."

"How?"

"I was junior pathologist at the time. I'd been in Thanet about a year. Amos was my boss." Clough meant Jenkinson. "He was amazing, someone to learn from. An old school examiner from a different generation. He smoked, shouted, terrorised."

Gray remembered the version of Jenkinson he'd seen only a few days ago. They were completely different people now.

"And he was brilliant too," continued Clough. "Fantastic in court, lawyers were in awe of him. If Jenkinson pronounced a judgement on a PM, it was accepted. He really should have worked in one of the big cities, on big cases."

"Why didn't he?"

"I asked once, he told me he liked being a huge fish in a tiny pond. All that authority – he was bloody difficult to work for. Although his standards were very high, he could be inconsistent. He had favourites; others were allowed to get away with stuff that I simply couldn't."

"Were you friends?"

"Friends?" Clough gave a bitter laugh. "He used to scare the crap out of me! He was more of a reluctant mentor."

"So, you didn't socialise?"

"We went to the pub together, but it wasn't like us now. Usually there was a group of colleagues, all there to listen as Jenkinson regaled us with past tales; either a PM or a court case where he'd given testimony."

"Did you like him?"

"Like?" Clough drank some of his apple juice. "That's not a word I'd use. I respected his mind and his abilities, but he wasn't an easy man to get along with. He treated people he considered his juniors or from a lower class as little more than tools."

"Including you, by the sound of it."

"Correct. Status was important to Jenkinson. At the beginning it didn't bother me, I was just happy to be learning from him. I played the inferior fiddle for a couple of years. It was okay until I realised how he was treating me and the team. I got more and more frustrated about being in the background. I'd joined the department to make a difference, yet I felt like I was only barely trusted to handle the basics. Learning, though slowly."

"Treated, how?"

"These days Jenkinson would be called out for bullying and harassment. He wouldn't have recognised those terms. He was from a different generation. Thankfully, those days are largely over."

Gray recognised this kind of behaviour from his time in the police, particularly his first years when he was in uniform. It was supposed to toughen you up and woe betide anyone who complained. As Clough had said, things were different now.

"What's this got to do with Jessop?"

"I'm coming to that. It was early summer, the beginning of June, and Amos had gone on holiday a couple of days previously. Up to Scotland for a week-long tour of the lochs. Another colleague, someone Jenkinson regularly turned to, was off sick. Meaning I was on call when her body was discovered. The sad thing is, looking back, although someone had died, my only emotion was excitement. Finally, a significant case to get my teeth into!"

"What do you remember from the scene?" asked Gray.

"Everything, it's like a graphic movie in my mind, Sol. The flat was on the second floor. The door stood open, half hanging off the hinges. Somebody had kicked it in. There was even a footprint on the wood. The eyes of the uniform cop at the entrance running over me. Pulling on the evidence suit, stepping inside.

"Along the corridor. Mike Fowler on the phone, talking to your old boss Jeff Carslake, watching me proceed as well. My palms were sweaty, my medical bag heavy. She lay in the living room, on her back; hair, legs and arms splayed. It was stiflingly hot, the radiator turned to full. A stench; of excrement and the beginnings of decomposition."

"How long had Zara gone undiscovered?"

"Body temperature is the best indicator though the rate of cooling depends on many factors. It can take anything from eight to thirty-six hours for a body to feel cold to the touch."

Gray held up a hand to interrupt Clough. "I know all this; I've been doing this long enough that I don't need an explanation."

"Sorry, you're right. Anyway, the heat in the room affected my assessment. And there was no rigor mortis. In a normal environment that would mean something like twelve hours after death, but more heat means faster rigor onset. So, it was difficult to be clear. Eventually, we settled on approximately two days. At least that's something Jenkinson agreed with."

"Cause of death you identified as blunt trauma."

Clough sighed. "That's what caused all the problems."

"Why?"

"Jenkinson."

"I don't understand."

"As I mentioned, he was on holiday and a more senior colleague was sick, so I took responsibility as the lead forensic pathologist."

"Understandable."

"You would think so, but later on that day I received a call from him. Jenkinson was absolutely furious with me for carrying out the PM. He said I should have rung. He slammed the phone down, broke off from his holiday and drove straight back to Thanet."

"What did you think to that?"

"He'd always possessed an explosive personality, but that felt somewhat extreme." It did to Gray as well. "He was in the following morning at the crack of dawn. When I arrived, he was very cold and calm. He'd already reviewed my notes and undertaken another PM."

"Isn't that unusual?"

"It's not uncommon for a second review to happen under certain circumstances, but usually it's as a result of the defence team at a trial trying to find a mistake the pathologist has made in order to get their client off their hook. This felt more like the boss not trusting the worker and checking for themselves. Particularly when he hauled me into his office and trashed my analysis. Although he agreed with my assessment that the cause was blunt trauma, he reckoned it was accidental death, severe inebriation being a significant contributing factor. I'd been less equivocal, and he didn't like that. I recall him shouting that pathologists should be definitive in their assessments to remove any margin of error in subsequent legal proceedings."

"Jenkinson's perspective is understandable. Blood and bone fragments were found on the fire surround and she had a high alcohol content in her body."

"At the time we didn't have any information on quite how inebriated she was because the test results weren't back. And no booze was visible at the crime scene."

"But the report states very clearly a bottle was found nearby."

"There wasn't a bottle when I was on site."

"So where was it?"

"The SIO, Mike Fowler, said he'd picked it up before my arrival and bagged it. And when the test results came in showing she was blind drunk that just confirmed Jenkinson's perspective on events." Clough sipped his drink. "The trouble was I couldn't see how she could have fallen. There weren't any trip hazards."

"But if she was that drunk, she could have simply collapsed."

"It seemed unnatural to me. However, Jenkinson overrode me on that aspect too."

"What about the inquest itself?"

"As I said, once Jenkinson returned, he took over everything, including the hearing. I wasn't involved at all."

"Did you look for anything else in the PM?"

"Like what?"

"Pregnancy?"

Clough paused before he said, "She'd clearly had a child, and recently."

"But that's not in your or Jenkinson's PM notes." Gray pushed the paperwork he'd brought with him across the table. The pathologist didn't even look at it. "This is the report we have on file and was presented as evidence at the inquest." Gray flipped the folder open. "That's your signature at the bottom, right?"

"Yes." Clough squirmed in his chair.

"What the hell is going on, Ben?"

"That's not what I originally wrote. It was altered."

"By who?"

"Me."

"Why?"

"I'm well aware of how it looks, Sol. Back then I was under the thrall of a very influential man who could make or break my career with a couple of well-placed phone calls."

"So, you were coerced?"

"I could say yes, however that would be an easy way of absolving myself of the responsibility. Jenkinson pushed me hard and I folded. I could have stood up to him, but I didn't. He'd have fired me; I'd have been out of a job and the report would still reflect Jenkinson's wishes. And, there was another complication, another lever Jenkinson could yank on." Clough twirled his glass on a coaster. "I'd started a relationship with his daughter. I was besotted with her and, she told me, she shared my feelings. Jenkinson, however, wasn't of the same mind. He didn't like it at all, in fact he hated us being together. We tried to keep our status very quiet. I never went around to meet the parents. Fiona was working full time for social services and had her own place."

"So, what happened?"

"He threatened my relationship with Fiona if I didn't do what I was told."

"How?"

"He said he had friends high up in the police who could hit me with a charge that would get me sent to prison."

"Such as?"

"Sex with an underage child." Clough shuddered. "I still remember his grinning face now. He told me how easy it would be. That he knew the perfect girl, or maybe even boy, and a willing cop or two. All would swear blind what I'd been up to. Even if the charges didn't stick it would be a smear I'd never escape."

"Good God."

"Therefore, I did what he wanted, and I've stayed quiet all the years since."

"Why change now?"

"Jenkinson's on his last legs."

"Did Fiona say anything about the state of Jenkinson's marriage?"

Clough frowned. "Why do you ask?"

"Just curious."

"Fiona doted on her mother, Millicent, I know that much. She died not long after we split up."

"When did you separate?"

Clough gave a short, derisive chuckle. "That's what makes all of this so ironic. It was shortly after the inquest, once matters were closed and buried."

"What caused the break-up?"

"I've no idea. I just received a letter in the mail, the old-fashioned way, telling me it was over. I was devastated, of course."

"Have you seen Fiona since?"

"Just the once, at a function. I spotted her across the room. I couldn't speak I was so knotted up inside. The way she looked at me." Clough shook his head. "Like I was shit on her shoe." Clough leant forward, elbows on the table, head in his hands. "What a mess."

"It's hard to disagree."

"If you need me to make a statement at any point I'll do so, of course. I'll accept my fate."

"For what?"

"Lying."

"Who's going to care now?"

"I do."

"Then you'll just have to learn to live it with again, Ben."

Gray left Clough alone with his thoughts.

Twenty Two

"And you've no idea who this older man, the father, might be?" asked DCI Hamson. She and Gray were together in her office, at the table in the corner.

"I'm not certain yet."

"What about Gordon Ogilvy?"

"The DNA results don't match. Gordon seems to just be a patsy."

"And Fowler was the SIO?"

"That's right." Several years back Hamson and Mike Fowler had been having an affair. Fowler was married at the time. Only Gray was in on their secret.

"Could it be Fowler?"

"Not a chance."

Hamson shook her head. "Do you think he altered the crime scene? To make it appear to be an accident?"

"It's impossible to tell at this stage. Maybe Clough really did miss the bottle. Maybe it really was there all along."

"Maybe."

Gray knew Hamson was thinking the same as him – when you knew somebody had broken the rules once you suspected them every time.

Like Worthington.

"We can discount the suspect being police," said Gray. Because every officer had to provide a DNA sample – in case they accidentally contaminated a crime scene. Therefore, the database would automatically have cross-referenced every officer. "But he had or has still a responsible role – whatever that would mean to a girl just seventeen years old."

"Who'd lived for a couple of years on the street and danced in a strip club, Sol. I'd bet she had a far more experience of life's hardships than most people twice her age."

"You're probably right," he admitted.

"What are you doing next?"

"There's no point in speaking with Amos Jenkinson, his mind is shot to pieces." And Fowler was gone too. "I'll go to the club where Zara worked. See if I can track down Lucy Gold, the friend mentioned in the crime scene report. But it's a long time ago."

"Eight years isn't all that much."

"Look how many people involved in this case have died. And memories fade fast."

"Not fast enough, sometimes." He guessed she meant Fowler. "Jesus, Sol."

"I know."

"Speaking of shadows from the past, Frank McGavin."

"What about him?" McGavin had been a significant player in the local underworld until he'd fled overseas to avoid arrest and had been hiding in plain sight ever since in Northern Cyprus, a region which didn't have an extradition treaty with the UK.

"The CPS have dropped all the charges."

"Why?"

"Insufficient evidence."

"That's ridiculous."

"The decision has been made." Hamson held her hands up.

"Can't the superintendent pull a few strings?"

"I've already tried that."

"There must be other avenues, surely?"

"Sol, I've tried my damndest. There's nothing can be done about it. McGavin has no case to answer, end of."

Gray leant his chair back on two legs. "Now what happens?"

"Nothing. McGavin is free to come home when he likes."

"He'll find the landscape very different to when he ran things."

"That's for sure."

"Anyway, I'll deal with McGavin if he returns."

"I'd say *when*, Sol. Not *if*."

Gray dropped the chair back onto all four legs and stood.

"There's one more thing."

"Oh?" He sat down again.

"You're not going to like it." Hamson picked up a pen, twiddled it between her fingers. "HR has decided not to get the PSD involved with Worthington."

"Why the hell not?"

"Just because he accessed their records doesn't mean Worthington was up to anything."

"They're just being weak, Von. Not wanting us to look bad in the public eye if another dirty cop gets the boot."

"The decision is made."

"Brilliant."

"Deal with it, Inspector. Anyway, it's late. I'm going home."

Gray paused at the top of the stairs, slammed the side of his fist against the wall. He wasn't letting Worthington off the hook. Not now.

He needed to make a call, but not here. Too many ears.

GRAY SAT IN HIS CAR and watched Hamson drive away. He pulled his phone out, tapped in the number but paused before pressing the green key. Was he sure he should contact someone he knew to be a criminal? Did Gray want justice, regardless of the cost?

He decided that when it came to Worthington, he did. He made the call.

"Who's this?" asked Andrew Abbott when he answered.

"We met in the hospital. We talked about your son, Eric, being assaulted."

"I remember, officer. I hope you've some good news for me?"

"I know who attacked your son."

"I'm listening," said Abbott.

Twenty Three

Gray waited in one of the shelters set into the cliffs on the Ramsgate esplanade. Cut into the cliffs by the Victorians, they'd been intended as genteel places to rest and take in the sea air. Now, the exterior was peeling paint, softening wood and cracked glass. Inside was a graffiti'd bench and a fair share of wind-blown detritus in the corners.

The tide was up, and the waves beat against the nearby concrete sea defence. This was never a busy area, even at the height of summer. The tourists tended to stick to the main beaches. This was a good half mile from the pubs and cafes of the Ramsgate seafront. In January, when the wind blew, there was the occasional dog walker, but that was it.

A few drops of rain hit the esplanade.

"Bit out the bloody way, isn't it?" Abbott stepped inside.

"That's kind of the point," said Gray. Abbott sat down. "How's Eric?"

"He's at home now, recovering." Abbott shifted on his backside, pivoted towards Gray, eyes narrowed into slits. "Who attacked my son?"

"A colleague."

"So, a cop?"

"That's right."

"And nothing is going to get done about it, that's why we're here?"

"You catch on fast, Abbott." Abbott stood, walked out onto the esplanade, glanced in both directions. "It's just me and you."

"I'm being careful." Abbott sat back down, focused on Gray. "Why would you help me?"

"My colleague's behaviour goes against everything I believe in."

"And you want me to sort him out? Like a vigilante? Doesn't that go against your code?"

"Do you want to know or not?"

"Course."

"Then stop questioning my motives."

Abbott shrugged. "Whatever, mate. Ultimately I don't care."

"You still have connections, right?"

"Oh, yeah," nodded Abbott. "Plenty. What's his name then?"

Gray held for a moment before he said, "Jerry Worthington." Then Gray told Abbott Worthington's address.

Abbott tapped the details into his phone, shoved it in his pocket. "I'll sort him."

Gray grabbed Abbott's arm. "We never met, all right?"

Abbott's grin was humourless. "I've done this before, don't worry." Then he left.

Gray stayed where he was, leaning back, legs outstretched, asking himself if he was bothered by his actions. He decided it was a resounding, *no*. Worthington had asked for this.

Outside the rain started properly. Big fat drops patterning the grey concrete. Gray waited for the weather to pass.

It always did.

Twenty Four

The Platinum Club was located in what appeared to be an old church on Cleaver Lane in the Eastcliff section of Ramsgate. The architecture – sloped roof, bell tower and dominant arched windows – certainly made it seem that way. However, the windows were bricked up now and the outside painted a summery yellow.

Cleaver Lane itself was very narrow and cobbled. Faded double yellow lines ran down either side and bollards spaced a few yards apart along the length separated it from the large, council run pay-and-display Staffordshire Street car park which served Ramsgate. Whatever industrial building had occupied this space was long gone. Houses backed onto the car park and, beyond, were the high rises of Kennedy House and in the other direction the spire of St. George's church.

The club opened evenings only. It advertised pole and lap dancing 'for the discerning gentleman'. When the place had first thrown its doors open something of a minor local media frenzy had occurred – people waving placards outside claiming the club would be a bad influence on their children, all watched by television cameras and the press. Gradually the furore died down. The campaigners drifted away, and other stories were of more interest.

So, the club was still here. Gray had visited twice in the past – to deal with the aftermath of an assault during the protests, then again, a few months later when Fowler dragged a group of colleagues around the area on a birthday night out – one of the rare events Gray attended.

Gray headed through the entrance, solid wooden doors giving no view of the interior which hadn't changed much, simply been given a refresh. The lobby was bright, light and open. A bar area tucked to one side, more doors straight in front leading to the dancing area and some stairs tucked behind a wall. Dull music throbbed.

A well-presented black woman possessing voluminous afro hair walked over to Gray. A short skirt exposed long legs and heels.

"Welcome to the Platinum experience." She smiled broadly. "I'm Brandi. What can I get you?"

"The manager, please." Gray showed his warrant card.

Brandi's grin didn't dim in the slightest. "I'll fetch her straight away." She disappeared upstairs.

A few moments later an equally tall woman, her hair long and dark, cut to a tight fringe above her eyes, came down the steps, Brandi close by. She wore a trouser suit and flat shoes. Gray handed over his warrant card again.

"Deborah Pinner," she said. "I'm the owner. I hope we haven't upset any of our neighbours."

"Not as far as I'm aware. Is there somewhere we can speak in private?"

"Come on up, Inspector." Pinner handed back his card before leading him up the stairs to her small office. "Do you want anything to drink?"

"No, thanks." Pinner sat in a high-backed chair behind her desk. "We're totally legitimate, fully licensed with all the right documentation."

"I'm sure you are."

"Council representatives visit regularly to ensure we comply. We insist on a no touch policy and our dancers must wear a thong, knickers or briefs at all times. I'm a businesswoman first and foremost. I've a fair chunk of my own money tied up in this building and I want it to succeed, so whatever you need I'll do my best to help."

Quite a little speech.

"I appreciate it," said Gray. "You've been open about a decade, right?"

"Correct. I'm sure you recall all the fuss."

"I do."

"There's the main section where members and guests can watch live shows and a more discrete area out the back for more intimate, one-on-one dance. I started off running clubs in London and moved down here with my husband and kids for a better life. The husband's gone now, but we're still kicking. My target audience is businessmen – preferably from the capital as they pay more. However, anybody with money is welcome." Pinner flashed a grin. "Provided they behave. My employees are my most important assets. Without them I'd have nothing. And without me they'd be earning a lot less. We're like a family. We all look out for each other."

"Sounds admirable, Miss Pinner."

"I like to think so."

"Eight years ago, a Zara Jessop was working here."

"That's not a name I remember off the top of my head. Then again, I've employed a lot of girls and guys over the years. Let me check. Our records are digitised." Pinner turned to her laptop. She focused on it briefly. "Of course, I recall her now. Here she is." Pinner tapped her screen. "She wasn't one of mine for long, just a few months." Pinner spun the laptop around. The photo on screen was indeed Zara. Clean, smiling – not the battered and ruined girl on the mugshot.

"That's her."

"She died, right?"

"Yes. Anything you can recall about when she worked here would be helpful."

"Not much, to be honest. I have a strong relationship with my staff, but friends we definitely are not. Sometimes I have to make tough decisions and a bit of perspective and distance are valuable. Eight years ago, we were still battling for acceptance and survival and I was going through a divorce. I had a lot on my plate. However," Pinner sat back. "Some of my current girls were here then. We can go down and talk to them if you'd like?"

"Is one Lucy Gold?"

"Actually, yes."

"And she's in the building now?"

"She should be. It's still quite early so we should be able to catch her. If you'd arrived an hour later, it might have been more of a challenge. Lucy is popular."

Gray followed Pinner out of the office and back down the stairs. She pulled open the doors into the main area of the club, a large open dimly lit space. The music was loud and thumping.

Separate tables and chairs were spread out through the area, all centred on a raised central stage shaped like a figure of eight, two long brass poles on either circle. At the moment the stage was empty and only a handful of chairs were occupied.

A waitress threaded her way between the tables, tray in hand. Beyond was a long bar, where a man stood, his back turned to Gray, wearing just trunks and they were skin tight, while a woman behind the bar pulled drinks.

Pinner pushed her way through a door marked 'Private' at the far edge of the dance area. Gray entered a brightly lit corridor. She headed into the first door they came to, paused in the entrance, said, "Wait here a moment please," before she disappeared inside. Moments later, Pinner was back. "I just wanted to check Lucy was all right first without barging through. Just in case she was in flagrante."

Inside was a changing area, long and narrow. Lockers against one wall, mirrors opposite, seats in front, more bright lights.

"Lucy Gold," said Pinner. "Detective Inspector Gray."

Gold sat facing a mirror. She was heavily tanned, more than likely fake at this time of year, had long, curly and very ginger hair. And she was topless, wearing just golden spangly knickers and high heels. She watched Gray closely. Perhaps this was her way of shocking him, maybe Pinner's too. Gold span around, crossed one leg over another.

"Hello," said Gray.

"Hello yourself," said Gold. "I understand you want to talk about Zara."

"That's right."

"We worked together for a few months, on the same shifts. We became quite close. She had a hell of a body on her, initially anyway."

"Did she tell you about herself?"

"In great detail. She'd run away from home and was living in some crappy flat nearby. She hated her family, except her brother, can't remember his name."

"Edgar."

"Oh, yes. In the early days I was interested in her, you know." Gold winked. "But I soon realised how nice she was and what a shit hand life had given her. Plus, she had her eye on someone else, the poor cow."

"Who?"

"A man who used to come here a lot. I'd given him a few private dances until Zara turned up, then all he wanted was her. Not that I blamed him, of course. I happily passed him to her. He was a good tipper and she needed the money."

"What was his name?"

Gold shrugged. "He didn't say, and I didn't ask. I could tell he was married, though, and more than likely had kids. Those kinds of guys don't say much about themselves. They turn up for the type of entertainment they're not getting at home. Two separate lives which don't intertwine." She winked at Gray.

"I wouldn't know."

"Course not."

"Why did Zara leave?"

"Cos of the baby bump."

"Once I learned she was pregnant," said Pinner, "I put Zara on maternity leave. We kept her job open, paid her a small wage so she would be all right. I couldn't afford much, but it would keep her off the streets. And if she wanted, she could return once sorted after the birth. She never did, though."

"Do you recognise either of these two men?" Gray showed photos stored on his phone. First, Gordon Ogilvy. Both women shook their heads. Fowler was next. He'd told Hamson Fowler couldn't be the father, but Gray wanted to be sure.

"Him I know," said Gold.

"Me too," said Pinner. "He's that cop who was in here all the time."

"Not for Zara, before you ask. Her fella was bigger than this guy."

"Why did he come, then?" asked Gray.

Gold laughed. "Same reason I told you earlier. Second life."

In Fowler's case it was third or maybe even fourth life. Gray asked, "After she left were you and Zara in contact again?"

"No," said Pinner.

"I was," said Gold. "Several times, right up until the baby was born. The last occasion we met in a café. Zara looked like she'd burst open right there if she wasn't careful. She was in a right mess, said the baby's father had dumped her. She didn't know how she was going to cope and was talking of having the baby adopted."

"God," said Pinner. "I had no idea."

"The report I read said it was you who called the police," said Gray.

"We were supposed to have another coffee together," said Pinner. "To meet her kid for the first time. Zara didn't turn up, didn't answer her phone, didn't respond to me banging on her door. I was there when your lot went in. Maybe if I'd have called earlier things would have been different."

"Very unlikely. I've read her post-mortem report. Zara fell and banged her head. She'd been dead a couple of days by then."

"That cop you showed me just now made me stay outside. When he told me, Zara was dead I couldn't believe it. I've often wondered if I could have done more to help." Gold wiped away a tear. Pinner grabbed a tissue from a nearby box, handed it to Gold who dabbed away at her eyes.

"What about the baby?"

"I did mention it. The cop said everything was being dealt with. He sent me away. Her funeral was a couple of weeks later. Most of the girls went. So did her brother, nobody else from her family. I couldn't believe her mum wasn't there. I don't know what I'd do without mine." Gold glanced up at the clock on the wall. "God, look at the time. I'd better fix my make-up then get out and mingle."

Gray passed over one of his cards. "If you think of anything else, please give me a call."

"I'll show you out, Inspector," said Pinner.

The dance area was busier than earlier. More tables taken, more chatter, same loud music.

At the front door Pinner said, "Feel free to come back any time, we'll be happy to entertain you."

"I'll keep it in mind."

As Gray walked back to the car his mobile rang. Fiona Jenkinson.

"Sol, hi." Fiona sniffed, sounded like she'd been crying.

"What's the matter?"

"I just wanted to let you know that Dad died this afternoon in his sleep."

"I'm so sorry."

"It's for the best. He's joined Mum now." Another sniff. "The funeral will be in a couple of days. I'll send you the details."

"That soon?"

"Before Dad got really bad, he insisted we make the arrangements. It's only simple anyway."

"If I can do anything, just let me know."

"Thanks, Sol. I'd better go."

"I'll come over if you want."

"I'm not ready right now."

"Okay."

"But thanks, I appreciate it." Fiona rang off.

Within moments Gray's mobile buzzed. A text from Vardie. "I've just found the Section 47 report I was supposed to send you lodged in my outbox. The file size was too large. I've sent it again, my apologies."

Gray had forgotten about that document. He opened it on his phone and read with a bit of difficulty – the text was small on the screen. He got to the end, went back to the beginning again.

The complaint was indeed about Gordon Ogilvy. The child's name wasn't stated. But what interested Gray was the date. The Section 47 had been served ten years ago, not eight. Well before Andrea stopped fostering.

Gray called Draper, said, "When we talked yesterday you mentioned your parents were subject to an enquiry and your mother stopped fostering as a result."

"Correct."

"Who told you that?"

"My mother. Dad was dead by then. Why?"

"I read some of the report just now. It's called a Section 47. The investigation actually occurred two years before your mother gave up fostering."

"Oh! That makes no sense."

"Your mother definitely made the link between the complaint and her no longer fostering?"

"Yes! I really don't understand."

"Okay, sorry to bother you." Gray disconnected. Draper's answers made Gray think of Kerry Hudson. Maybe there was a connection between her and Andrea.

He started the engine and drove to Hudson's house in Garlinge. It was late, but his questions needed answering.

He knocked on the door, but nobody answered. The lights were off, no car parked on the drive. She must be out for the night. And he didn't have her mobile number. He swore.

The questions would have to wait.

Twenty Five

The following morning Gray waited in his car, tapping his fingers impatiently on the steering wheel. He'd called Hudson's employer, Robson and Edwards, as soon as they'd opened and been told that she was showing a house on Dickens Road in Broadstairs. After some insistence on Gray's behalf the estate agents gave out Hudson's phone number but when he called, it diverted straight to voicemail.

Gray drove over, pulled up outside across the drive. There was a 'For Sale' sign in the small front garden. Parking here was tight. Few of the residences possessed drives and the beach was just a few hundred yards away so tourists used the roads around here too.

When the door opened, Gray got out, leaned against the front wing. The sound of the breaking waves carried to him easily. The wind was up. Hudson followed out the couple she was showing the property to, pulled the door closed behind her. When she turned back, she caught sight of Gray and paused mid-speech. The man and woman glanced at him. He walked over to the trio.

"Sorry, what?" asked Hudson.

"We were asking about the schools around here," said the man as he buttoned up his coat over a suit.

"They're fine."

"That's it?" asked the woman.

"How old are your children?" asked Gray. The man frowned at him. "My kids went to school here so I can help answer your question." Gray showed his warrant card.

"We've got twins, they're thirteen." The man still sounded suspicious.

"Then I'd suggest going for Dane Court, it's a selective Grammar a few miles up the road."

"We were thinking of going private."

"Ah, then I can't help you. My wages never stretched that far."

The man didn't respond. He turned to Hudson. "We'd better be going."

"Okay, well thanks for letting me show you around." Hudson shook both their hands in turn. "If I can tell you anything else, please just call me."

"Would you mind moving your car," said the man. "We need to get out."

Gray nearly pointed out he'd failed to use the word please. "Happy to, sir." He reversed into the road, leaving enough room for the man to back his Volvo out and drive away. Gray regained his space. Hudson was waiting for him.

"They were a pleasant couple," said Gray. "DFLs, I guess?" A local acronym – Down From London. Thanet, and Broadstairs in particular, was becoming increasingly popular with families moving out of the capital and using their equity to buy a far bigger home by the sea. The wage earners continued to work in London, commuting by train each day. When the journey time was well over two hours for a distance of around eighty miles the DFLs were few and far between. Now, with the timespan slashed back to little more than an hour, the exodus from the capital was in full flow. Broadstairs was regularly in the newspapers as a place to relocate away from the bustle of big cities.

"What is this, Inspector?" asked Hudson, ignoring Gray's question. "Why are you tracking me down while I'm working?"

"I've got some more questions."

"I haven't got the time right now; I have another showing in a few minutes."

"You don't. I spoke to your office. I know you've got at least an hour free."

"There's paperwork to do."

"It'll have to wait. Let's walk." Gray pointed towards the cliffs. He turned at the bottom of the road, along Eastern Esplanade, heading away from Broadstairs past three- and four-storey houses with great sea views. They walked next to the cliff edge, protected from the drop by metal railings.

"What can you tell me about Andrea Ogilvy?"

"She was a bloody life saver, Inspector. She really turned my life around. There wasn't a bad bone in that woman's body."

"Did you go to her funeral?"

"Of course. Lots of her children did."

"Is that how you see yourselves?"

"I'm an orphan, I don't know who my real parents are. I moved around quite a few homes. It wasn't pleasant. Andrea and Gordon had faith in me when nobody else did. I owe them everything."

"Do you remember another girl who the Ogilvy's fostered; Zara Jessop?"

"Our paths crossed when she lived with Andrea for a few months. Zara was one messed up girl. From a really good background, not like mine at all."

"Were you friends?"

"Not really."

"Why?"

"As I said, our backgrounds were very different. Zara thought of herself as better than me. She was quite a trouble causer too and made life difficult for both Gordon and Andrea."

"And Fiona Jenkinson?"

"Of course. She was round all the time."

"Would you say she was good friends with the Ogilvy's?"

"She came for dinner quite often and they seemed to laugh together a lot. Fiona even brought her boyfriend a few times. Nice guy, cold hands, though."

"Do you remember his name?"

"Ben."

"Clough?"

"Maybe, I'm not sure."

"Have you heard of a Section 47?"

"Means nothing to me."

"You said Gordon and Andrea were very important to you."

"Absolutely."

"So why did you complain about Gordon to Social Services?"

Hudson stopped in her tracks, stared at Gray. "Excuse me?"

"I read an investigation report carried out by them stating you had issues with Gordon Ogilvy."

"Like what, specifically?"

"Like he propositioned you."

"That's ridiculous! When was this supposed to have occurred?"

"Before you moved out."

"Never, ever happened." Hudson shook her head.

"The report says otherwise. And there was a period of about a year between the apparent events and you reporting them."

"I didn't *report* anything."

"Zara Jessop made the complaint first. Social services then approached other girls for confirmation."

"Somebody is lying." Hudson leant back against the fence; her arms crossed. "Was this complaint the Section 47 document you referred to?"

"Yes."

"And did it happen to be raised at the time Andrea stopped fostering?"

"It appears to be the cause of her putting an end to her work."

"Jesus. This explains everything now." Hudson bowed her head, rubbed at the bridge of her nose. Gray waited until Hudson eventually said, "I'd moved out by the time this all happened. I had a call from one of my friends who'd been with Andrea too. She told me that Andrea was giving up looking after children. None of us could believe it.

"I went round. She asked me if anything had happened with Gordon. I asked what she meant but she just smiled and told me to forget what she'd said."

"So, Andrea never told you anything? Didn't say why she stopped her work?"

"Not a thing."

"Why do you think you'd be named in a complaint?"

"I've no idea." Hudson sounded suddenly tired. "Look, I don't feel like speaking about this anymore, Inspector."

"All right. I may be in touch again if something else arises, okay?"

"Fine. But let me tell you one thing for sure. I'd never do anything to hurt the Ogilvy's. Besides my fiancée they've been the best people in my life." Hudson stared at Gray for a long moment before she turned and walked away. Gray watched her retreat, wondering who'd lied.

WHEN GRAY GOT TO THE station Ibbotson came in. "Can you talk, sir?" he asked.

"Sure."

"DC Worthington wasn't due to be off work today, right?"

"Not to my knowledge."

"Have you seen him?"

"I've only just arrived. Why do you ask?"

"He's not turned up for his shift and he's not answering his phone. He doesn't have a holiday booked and hasn't called in sick."

"Go round and visit him then."

"Just did. There was no answer. I hammered on his door several times."

"Maybe he's staying with somebody else?" Or perhaps Abbott had been round to have that word with Worthington already.

"Maybe." Ibbotson didn't sound convinced.

"I don't know what else to suggest, Ted."

"I'm concerned, sir."

"So am I, sergeant. We're another officer down when we're already short of manpower. And, as usual, it's DC Worthington who's the culprit."

Ibbotson pushed the office door shut. "Sir, do you mind if I speak plainly?"

"Go ahead."

"It's because of you he's been off."

"Now wait a minute, sergeant, he has himself to blame for that."

"You're biased against him."

"We've had this conversation already. Unless you've got anything valuable to add I'm throwing you out because I need to get on."

"Sir."

"Well, do you?"

"I'll keep looking for him."

"No, I want you here in the station doing some real work. When Worthington actually turns up, we'll find out then what's been going on."

Gray's internal phone rang.

Sergeant Morgan on the front desk. "Sol?"

"Is it quick?"

"You've got a visitor. An interesting one."

"I'll be down in a minute." Gray returned his attention to Ibbotson. "Have you got that?"

"Yes, sir."

"First sensible thing you've said."

Ibbotson left.

Gray headed down to the front desk. His visitor certainly was interesting.

Twenty Six

"You said to get in touch if I thought of anything else," said Lucy Gold as he showed her into an interview room. She wore jeans and a tight t-shirt beneath a denim jacket. "Have you seen today's paper?"

"Which one?"

"The Gazette."

"Is that even sold any more?"

"It's gone online, Inspector." At least Gold didn't roll her eyes.

"One second." Gray brought up a web browser on his phone, tapped in Thanet Gazette. The local newspaper was long gone. It used to be delivered to every house in the area for free. But as advertising moved online the profitability of the newspaper plummeted and the paper itself went digital only, merged into a general mess of Kent based publications. "What am I looking at?"

"There's a picture of the old guy that Zara used to see."

"Where?"

"Give it here." Gold snatched his phone and prodded away at it several times before she handed it back. "This guy getting cremated tomorrow, he was Zara's boyfriend."

Amos Jenkinson.

There was a photo, taken maybe a decade ago, selected presumably because it showed the man before the disease. The article underneath was short, simply stating Jenkinson was to be cremated in a private ceremony, then followed a brief biography about Jenkinson's role as Thanet's forensic pathologist, which was why he'd made it into the news, and finally a sentence stating that any donations for flowers were to be sent to a local charity.

"It can't be."

"I swear on my mother's life, that's him."

"Good God. Will you make a statement to that effect?"

"Now?"

"Please."

"If it helps, sure. Speaking to you made me think about Zara a lot last night."

"Wait here, I'll get someone in as soon as I can."

Gray couldn't believe it. But how to prove Lucy's claim? Gray would need clear and irrefutable evidence. He picked up his mobile, placed a call.

"Fiona? It's Sol. I'd like to come round and see you to pay my respects."

Twenty Seven

They were sitting in the kitchen; Fiona had made herself a cup of tea. Nothing for Gray.

"His car leaves the funeral directors for a 9.15am service at the Margate Crematorium in two days."

"Can I visit him?"

Fiona shook her head. "The casket is already closed."

Gray could get a warrant to access Jenkinson's corpse and obtain some DNA. But if he was wrong, if Jenkinson wasn't the father of the baby in the box and he made a huge fuss...

Fiona continued, "I'll be standing outside to watch the car enter the crematorium, but that's it. You're welcome to join me if you wish."

Gray didn't really see the point. "The arrangements are unusual."

"It's how Dad wanted it to happen." Fiona stared into her tea, frowned. "Other people's wishes were never really his consideration. Pathologists, they're a selfish bunch. He'd be in and out at all times of the day when he was working. Called off across the country to be performing post-mortems. He was more interested in the dead than the living." Then she looked up, forced a grin, tears in her eyes. "Anyway, we're all in a better place now."

"Is that why you and Ben Clough split?"

"I haven't thought about Ben in years." She seemed lost in her memories for a few moments. "How did you know about him and me?"

"I learned from him about your father having cancer. He said you two used to be in a relationship."

"It was nothing, just a brief fling." She brushed the comment away. "He wasn't the man for me, unfortunately."

"How about you? How are you doing?"

"The house feels empty without Dad," said Fiona. "It's all very strange. Anyway, I'll get the house cleared then put it on the market. I can finally get on with my life again."

"Good to hear. Look, I didn't want to intrude."

"Well, thanks for coming."

"Do you mind if I use your toilet first?" asked Gray.

"Of course. It's just down the hall." Fiona pointed, took her mug to the sink.

Gray pulled the kitchen door to and went along the hall to the bathroom he'd seen when he was here before. The facilities were avocado green – a toilet, sink and soap, a cabinet on the wall. Toilet paper, a radiator.

But not the hairbrush he wanted.

Gray went back the way he'd come, paused outside the kitchen, heard the tap still running. He took the stairs, halted on the landing, pushed open the nearest door. Right first time. A larger bathroom in the same green coloured ceramic, shower behind a curtain.

On the sink was a glass with two toothbrushes. Gray didn't know which would be Jenkinson's and taking one would be obvious. There was a razor too, a cheap disposable of blue plastic with a clear cover over the blade.

Gray wondered how Fiona would have managed to shave Jenkinson at all, he imagined it to be a challenging task. There was stubble in the razor, of course, but the shaft of hair possessed much less genetic information. For testing Gray needed the follicle to be intact and that was why he wanted the brush, or a comb.

Not one here, either.

He headed back onto the landing, listened briefly for Fiona. Heard nothing. Next, he tried each door on the landing in turn, turning the handles quietly and carefully. He found Jenkinson's on the third attempt, but the seconds were ticking by and Fiona was bound to start wondering what the hell Gray was up to.

The curtains were drawn, the interior gloomy, smelling of must and sweat. The large double bed was neatly made. Either side were bedside cabinets, a reading lamp on both. In front of the window was a set of drawers, and a large three-piece mirror mounted atop, organised for dressing.

On the drawers were two collection of bottles; perfumes and lotions to one side, presumably once used by Jenkinson's deceased wife and not cleared away, aftershave and deodorant on the other.

There was also a brush and a comb set lying on a tray. Gray went for the brush, picked it up. There were several hairs stuck within. Gray took a glass vial and pair of tweezers out of his pocket. After removing the vial lid, he carefully withdrew several hairs from the brush and slid them inside the vial then the vial back in his pocket.

He left the room, closed the door carefully, made his way back to the stairs. Was outside the bathroom when Fiona said,

"What are you doing, Sol?" She'd paused halfway, one hand on the bannister, frowning.

"I couldn't find a towel to dry my hands with," said Gray. "So, I came upstairs."

"I'll see you out."

"No need."

"I insist, so you don't end up wandering around again."

Gray forced a laugh. Fiona didn't.

She stood at the door until Gray got into his car. He started the engine, placed a call. As he drove away, he saw Fiona through the window, standing back in the shadows, watching him.

The call was answered. Gray said, "Dr Aplin, I've got a hair sample for you which I'll be sending by courier. I'd appreciate you processing it as fast as you can."

"My pleasure," said Aplin.

When he was on the main road heading north east back to Margate, Gray rang Draper. "Can I look around your mother's house again? As long as it's no trouble."

"It feels like a never-ending job," she said. "I'll be there tonight after work. Is that all right?"

"See you then."

"ARE YOU OKAY, SOL?" Wyatt, standing in his office doorway.

"I'm fine." Gray forced a smile.

Clearly, Wyatt didn't believe him. She said, "Do you fancy popping out for something to eat?"

"The staff canteen?"

Wyatt pulled a face. "I was thinking of somewhere a bit more upmarket with actual edible food."

"Sure, why not?"

GRAY AND WYATT SAT side by side on the Margate concrete sea defence, a series of levels laid out like large steps. Opposite a handful of fishing boats were moored, beyond stood the protective harbour arm. To their right stood the concrete block of the Turner Contemporary gallery. The sun was out, and it was cold, a breeze coming off the sea, but equally the chill woke Gray up, enlivened him.

"These are pretty good," said Wyatt, bobbing a wooden fork into a bag of chips they were sharing. She'd suggested the café at the bottom of the hill from the station on the edge of the old town, but Gray had dragged her into the fish and chip shop next door, then brought her across the road and onto the beach.

"Told you."

Gray liked plenty of vinegar and salt on his, whereas Wyatt preferred them plain, so they'd roughly split the chips in half. A few feet away a large black backed gull eyed their food. Gray threw a stone but the gull nonchalantly avoided the pitch. Wyatt laughed at Gray's rubbish attempt, sipped some coffee from a Styrofoam cup.

"This is fantastic," said Wyatt. "It's nice to spend some time together."

"Thanks for coming down, I was struggling to maintain my focus this afternoon." Gray dropped his voice. "I know who the father of the baby in the box is."

Wyatt turned to him. The chip she was holding went back into the bag. "It sounds like this is going to be a problem."

"It's Amos Jenkinson. Used to be the district forensic pathologist before Clough. He was married and much older than the mother. He died only a day or so ago."

"God."

"There's worse. I think his daughter, Fiona, might have known what he'd done and kept it hushed up."

Wyatt frowned for a moment. "Bit of a scandal, I can sort of understand why."

"I'm wondering whether she was involved with the baby too."

"How so?"

"It's evidence, right?"

"Jesus, Sol. That's heartless."

"I didn't mean it that way, just that the baby was proof of Jenkinson's association with Zara."

"Association? God, this gets worse!"

"Hear me out. Fiona was a social worker involved with rehoming and fostering children and babies. She regularly went to the house where the baby in the box was discovered. Perhaps she persuaded Zara to give the child up and took it to Andrea while she figured out the next steps."

"But the baby died."

"Right, and when I first discussed the baby with Fiona, I think she was genuinely shocked about the discovery. She didn't expect it."

"What about the mother?"

"Zara, she died, accidentally according to the reports. Fell over and banged her head. Large amounts of alcohol in her body."

"But you've got proof now, that Jenkinson was the father," said Wyatt. Gray didn't answer. "Sol?"

"Nearly."

"Nearly?"

"I'm waiting for the results. That's why I'm jittery. And what I have isn't admissible." Wyatt gave Gray a flat look. "I took a hair from Jenkinson's bathroom without his daughter's consent." Wyatt put her head in her hands. "I didn't have any choice."

"You always say that."

"I was pretty sure Fiona wouldn't voluntarily help; I need to know first for sure before I make my next move."

"And once you have that information?"

"I'm going to have to force the issue."

"And people may get hurt?"

"They usually do."

"When the game is played by Solomon Gray's rules, at least."

Gray didn't have a comeback so they ate the rest of the chips in silence, watching the waves roll in.

Twenty Eight

The rain started as Gray got out of his car. He couldn't get near Andrea Ogilvy's place; the square was full of cars. People home from work, living in houses built when horses were the main mode of transport. He'd been forced to park on Oaklands Avenue, near the doctor's surgery, itself a vehicular pinch point.

Gray cut down Tippledore Lane, an ancient footpath which once connected St. Peter's church with the cathedral in Canterbury, here long before even the houses.

Where the lane emerged onto Ranelagh Grove he turned right, walked the few remaining yards. The 'For Sale' sign in the front garden had been replaced with 'Sold'. As predicted, houses didn't stay on the market for long round here. He knocked on the front door, tried to shelter from the rain in the narrow archway until Draper opened up. She was wearing dungarees, her hair held back by a bandana, a smudge of dirt across one cheek.

"God, sorry, come in," said Draper. She grabbed Gray's arm, tugged him inside like he needed the impetus. She slammed the door behind him, then sneezed, wiped her nose on the back of her hand. "It's the dust in this place."

"How's it going? The clearance, I mean." Gray had done it himself, for a father he barely knew.

"Slowly. Philip isn't willing to help. He finds it too painful. Apparently just being here reminds him we're orphans now." Draper rolled her eyes. "Like it's easy for me. However, I'm finding it cathartic. It's only stuff, things my parents bought or were given. I'm beginning to see it as a fresh beginning." She sounded just like Fiona. "And the house is sold, as you probably saw, so I have to get a move on."

"Do you want a cup of tea?" Draper hiked a thumb over her shoulder towards the kitchen. "I can put the kettle on."

Everyone wanted to offer him a drink.

"I'm fine, thanks."

"Let's go into the front room. My feet are killing me." Draper flopped into a large, comfy looking armchair leaving the sofa for Gray. One end was stacked up with a pile of photos in frames. "What can I do for you?"

"I wanted to ask you about one of the foster children who stayed here."

The paintings and mirrors were down off the walls now, standing on the floor, leant up. The photos likewise. More were butted up together on one end of the sofa.

"Do you remember Zara Jessop?"

"Zara?" Draper leaned forward, rested her arms on her thighs. "Why?"

"She's the mummified baby's mother."

"Jesus." Draper sat back; her mouth partly open. She shook her head. "Are you sure?"

"We have conclusive DNA evidence."

"I can't believe it."

"I'm telling you this in confidence."

"Nobody will hear it from me."

"She lived here a couple of times; I understand."

"I came across her photo only a few minutes ago, that's why I was so surprised when you asked. How weird is that?" Draper stood up, went to the pile next to Gray, flipped through them like you would records in a store. About a third of the way in she stopped, handed Gray the picture. "Here you go." She sat down.

Gray saw a serious-looking girl. Long brown hair, tucked behind one ear, staring impassively through the lens. "What are your memories of her?"

Draper blew air out from pursed lips. "She was what, just seventeen, when she came here with an attitude big enough to fill this room. Young, but acted old. Like she'd seen lots of stuff kids her age had no business to see. Not unusual for someone who'd been living on the street, from what I've experienced. She was very strong, very sure of herself, even at that age."

"Did you spend much time with her?"

"Not at all, she was a couple of years younger than me. I was in first year of university. I was hardly going to knock around with a schoolkid."

"What about Philip?"

"He was in full time employment. When he came back after getting his degree, he started a job straightaway and got his own place, so I don't think they ever met. Philip was long sick of sharing his life with strangers by then."

"Was there any trouble with her?"

"What kind?"

"Anything."

"Well, it wasn't her who defecated in Philip's drawer, if that's what you mean." Draper grinned. "I didn't hear Mum complaining of any significant problems." She shrugged. "No more than anyone else from a difficult background."

"Did she ever talk about her home or parents?"

"I asked once, when I was back for a weekend. She told me never to again, so I didn't. She was generally okay. My mum liked her, that's all, really."

Gray glanced again at the photo.

Draper held out her hand. "I'll put it back."

"That's all right. I'm nearer." Gray leaned over, paused. The next photo in the pile, an image in a gilt silver frame, caught his eye. It was larger and grander than the rest. He put Zara's down, picked the other up, peered closer. Three people posing for the camera. From the easy familiarity of the body language it was clear the trio knew each other well.

Andrea Ogilvy, two people bracing her. A woman, her hair long and black with touches of grey developing, tumbling past her shoulders one side, and a tall, distinguished-looking man the other.

Fiona and Amos Jenkinson.

Gray turned the picture round to Draper.

"Oh, Fiona" Draper pulled a sour face. "She was here all the time. Mum's social worker."

"How well would she have known Zara Jessop?"

Draper blinked, like Gray had asked a stupid question. "Very well indeed. I'm pretty certain Fiona brought Zara here."

"You didn't seem pleased I brought Fiona up."

"Not particularly. She wasn't invited to Mum's funeral."

"Why?"

"The photo was taken a while ago. It used to be on the mantlepiece, then it wasn't. I hadn't realised until now. I found it tucked in that cupboard over there. And to answer your question, Mum didn't want Fiona at the funeral. She specifically told me that before she died.

"She said they'd had a falling out but wouldn't say over what. Which was strange as Mum told me most things. I've been thinking a lot about the section 47 notice. Maybe it was Fiona who served the document? I do remember Mum being upset that people she thought highly of backed away and didn't support her. Mum stopped doing what she'd loved, and Fiona never had a reason to come around again. Maybe that was the problem with Fiona?"

"I don't know."

"I'm sorry I can't be more helpful."

Gray stood. "You've been great, thanks."

"If there's anything else I can do, just let me know." At the front door she said, "You never told me who the father of the baby in the box was."

"We're not sure yet." Which wasn't a lie.

She opened the door wide, let Gray step into the rain. He paused, one foot out, the other in. A man stood under an umbrella on the other side of the road, his back to the church. "Are you all right?" asked Draper.

Gray twisted round. "I'm fine. Thanks again for your time."

Draper glanced over Gray's shoulder, then back to him. "See you." She closed the door. When Gray turned around Frank McGavin was getting into the rear of a car. The door slammed shut.

The car accelerated away leaving Gray standing.

GRAY HAD JUST STARTED his engine when his phone rang.

"Inspector, it's Doctor Aplin from the PFA labs."

"You're working late."

"I wanted to crack on with the tests on the hair sample you sent. I have the data in front of me. The subject you took the sample from is the father."

"You're sure?"

"It's a match with a probability of 99.9%."

"That's good enough for me."

"I'll email you a report over shortly."

"Thanks for letting me know."

"Good luck."

Gray disconnected. He felt mixed emotions. He hadn't wanted to be right, but at least he was beginning to get some answers.

He got a text then. Abbott. "We need to talk. Same place. Now."

Rather than turning for home Gray made his way towards Ramsgate.

Twenty Nine

It was as dark as coal on the esplanade, no artificial illumination and hardly any natural light. Gray picked his way along the concrete sea defence, using the torch app on his phone to guide his way. The beam spread wide, illuminating a space in front of him.

To one side was a steep drop to the beach. But Gray could only hear the waves, the sea lost in the darkness. To the other side stood the towering chalk cliffs.

Abbott wasn't in the same shelter at the foot of the Ramsgate cliffs as last time. Another couple were there instead, in a grasp, mouths on each other.

"Hey!" shouted the man when Gray shone the beam inside.

"Sorry."

"Bloody perv." Then he was back on the woman.

The next shelter was empty. Gray found Abbott in the third.

"Your information was total crap." Abbott was seated, leaning forward, arms on thighs, chewing gum furiously. "It wasn't him."

Gray blinked. "You're wrong, it must be." He sat down a few feet from Abbott, trying to process what Abbott had said.

"I'm telling you, that Geordie bastard *wasn't* the one who set the dog on my lad."

"Are you sure?"

"Look, mate. You're really pissing me off now. I'm certain. We gave him a good going over. If it was him, he'd have spat, believe me. So, I beat up a cop for nothing."'

Gray leant back a pressure building up in his chest and a pounding headache coming on. "Did he see you?"

"What do you think I am, stupid? No, he didn't see me. Or anyone else. Don't worry, he won't make any connection you."

"Thank God for that." Gray released a lungful of air he'd been holding on to.

"Who's the next suspect on your list, Inspector? Or are you expecting me to randomly smack people around until I chance upon the right one?"

"I don't know."

"That's not a good answer." Abbott stood, a large shape in the shelter entrance. "Get in touch when you do know."

"I don't think so. I won't be contacting again."

"What was I then? A convenient enforcer?" Abbott shifted forward a step, looming over Gray. He shuffled sideways along the seat, trying to distance himself from Abbott.

He felt a tingle of fear. How had he got himself in this situation? "I made a big mistake," admitted Gray. Abbott moved suddenly, pressing his weight down onto Gray, a hand around his throat. Abbott's mouth was near Gray's face. "I've literally got your number, Inspector Gray. What would your boss think if we had a little chat about you?"

Gray tried to speak but couldn't. His hands clawed at Abbott, but the other man had the leverage. Then the pressure was released, Abbott upright again. Gray sucked in air.

"It's a good job one of us has a plan," said Abbott and left.

Gray waited a few minutes, allowing his heart rate to steady. If it wasn't Worthington who'd accessed the PNC to check out the kids, then who was it? Gray knew for sure it had to be a cop. But who? And what was the plan Abbott referred to?

Gray ignored the couple in the other shelter when walked back along the esplanade towards the distant streetlamps. As he neared the concrete strip's end his phone rang.

"Sir," Ibbotson said. "We've found Worthington."

Gray swallowed, his throat sore. "Which pub was he in?" Trying to sound light-hearted.

"Not quite, sir. He's in the hospital."

WORTHINGTON WAS PROPPED up in bed in a private room off a corridor in the QEQM. He was battered, bruised, one eye closed over, the other a slit.

"How are you doing, Jerry?" asked Ibbotson, his tone grave.

"All right," said Worthington. He spoke through puffy lips, affecting his enunciation.

"See I got you a room? Better than being stuck in the ward with a load of old blokes, right?"

"Nice one."

Ibbotson poured a glass of water for him, then paused. "I'll get you a straw."

"What happened?" asked Gray once Ibbotson had left.

"Two guys wearing masks jumped me as I was walking back from a night out. Thought I'd have a few beers before I returned, faced any more shit from you, boss." A chuckle which morphed into a cough. "They bundled me into the boot of a car, drove me to a warehouse."

"Where?"

"No idea. They tied me to a chair and beat me up."

"Why?"

"Maybe they didn't appreciate my good looks. Like that bloke in *Fight Club*."

Gray didn't know what Worthington was on about. "Go on."

"Once they'd hit me a few times they asked about a dog being set on some kids. Reckoned it was me what did it. I told them over and over, it weren't. They didn't believe us at first, so they kept hitting us. Cracked a rib, eventually. Then I blacked out. Where's bloody Ted with that straw?"

Gray passed Worthington the plastic cup. He held it between shaking hands, spilled more down himself than went into his mouth. "Thanks."

"Then what?"

"When I woke up, I realised I were in the boot of the car again. They dumped me outside me house and drove off. I called an ambulance and ended up here."

"That's everything?"

"Aye. They just asked about the dog attack. I couldn't tell them anything and eventually they must have realised I knew nowt, then got rid of me."

"We'll, you're safe now. Did you recognise them? Anything to identify them?"

"Not a bloody thing. Faces covered, long sleeves so no visible tats. They had gloves on. Accents were southern but can't pinpoint them. Youse lot all sound the same. All I know is, they knew what they were doing. This weren't their first beating." Worthington had another drink, passed the cup back. "You know what were weird? There was this guy, stood back in the shadows, watching it all. Big bastard, leaning on a cane. Didn't move, didn't say a word."

Jesus. *McGavin?*

"Did you recognise him?"

"Never seen him before." Ibbotson came in then. "'Bout bloody time."

"Sorry," said Ibbotson. "I had to go all the way to the canteen. It's a maze this place."

"All right," said Gray. "Get some rest. I'll send someone over to take a statement."

"Lot of bloody good that'll do," said Worthington.

"Worth a try," lied Gray.

"Obviously I won't be in for a few days."

"Do your best, Jerry. It's not like you've got cancer or anything."

Worthington just glared at him.

Thirty

In the corridor, the door closed, Gray thought back to what he'd said to Worthington just now.

It's not like you've got cancer or anything.

A throwaway comment that sparked something inside Gray.

He remembered Fiona telling him about Jenkinson's cancer. From experience he knew the hospital kept test samples as routine so they could make future cross comparisons. Therefore, the hospital would have Jenkinson's DNA.

Not long ago Gray had recovered from cancer. The Sri Lankan who'd treated him then was called Doctor Manesh. As a consultant Gray doubted Manesh would be here at this time, their hours were more sociable, but it was worth a try. Once Gray had orientated himself with a map he easily found the consultant's office. He'd been there enough times himself. As he'd expected though the door was locked and the light off.

"SOL," SAID FIONA AFTER she opened the door. "I wasn't expecting you."

"I was just passing," lied Gray. "Can I come in?"

"I was just about to go to bed."

"I won't keep you long."

After a moment's hesitation Fiona stepped out of the way to allow Gray entrance. She led Gray into the kitchen, leant on one of the cabinets like she needed the support.

"How can I help?" she asked. No offer of a drink this time.

"Have you heard of a Zara Jessop?"

Fiona blinked. "Who?"

Gray showed her a photo on his phone, taken just before Zara died. "She ran away from home several times and was fostered by Andrea."

Fiona stared intently at the image. "When would this have been?"

"Eight years ago."

"A long time." Fiona held the phone out for Gray to take back.

"So, do you recognise her?"

"Not really. I don't think she was one of mine." Fiona frowned, like she was thinking. "But Social Services will have the records. They'll be able to confirm. Sorry I can't be more helpful."

"I've already checked." Fiona blinked at Gray. "I believe the baby in the box was your father's."

"What?"

"You and the baby in the box. I believe you have the same father. You're half-sisters."

Fiona burst out laughing. "How ridiculous!" She laughed again. Gray didn't. "What makes you think so?"

"Some evidence I'm not at liberty to share."

Colour started to reach Fiona's cheeks. "You're saying my father impregnated a child who was under the age of consent?"

"Zara was seventeen when she got pregnant."

"Oh, well, that's all right then!" Fiona threw her arms up in the air. "Jesus! Seventeen?" She leant on the work surface, narrowed her eyes. "Why are you telling me this?"

"I'd like your permission to take a DNA sample for analysis."

"I thought you said my father was the baby's too?"

"I don't know for sure. Your DNA would confirm it."

"And if you get corroboration, what would you do with the result?"

"Inform her family."

"And what about the press? The papers are all over the story."

"Nothing would be said to them."

"Can you guarantee that?"

"As much as I can."

"That's not enough, Sol! Even if he was the baby's father, which I don't believe for even one second, why should his name be dragged through the mud? He was a good man!"

"I don't want to destroy anyone's reputation."

"But don't you see? That's exactly what would happen! And what for? She's dead, the baby's dead! Nobody wins!"

"Her family should know what happened to her."

"So fucking what? Why does her family count more than mine?"

"It's what's morally right, Fiona."

"Who gets to choose what's right or wrong? You? God?" Fiona shook her head. "The answer is no. Now get out of my house." Fiona pointed towards the front door."

"Fiona, if—"

"Leave." She strode over, pushed at Gray to get him to move. "And don't ever come back."

Gray raised his hands in surrender. "All right." He walked along the corridor, Fiona on his heels. He opened the door, stepped outside.

She slammed the door behind him.

Thirty One

"Where the bloody hell are you, Von?" said Gray to himself.

He pulled off the single road into a gap supposed to be used to allow cars to pass. To one side was a field, to the other a high hedge. Even though the ancient walled town of Sandwich was nearby it felt like he was in the middle of nowhere. There were no streetlights, so the tarmac stretched off into darkness. Gray didn't like it, give him obvious civilisation every day.

Hamson had told him she had a house in a tiny scattered settlement near Finglesham. Gray assumed he'd recognise her car parked on a drive as he went past, but no luck. Everything was far more spread out than he'd realised. There was no reason to come to Finglesham, unless you had to.

He pulled out his phone. There was only one bar of reception out here. Then even that dropped out. He got out of the car. In the distance an owl hooted, but otherwise it was silence. He walked around; phone held high in the air until the connection came back in again. He stayed still, dialled Hamson. "Von, it's Sol."

"I know," said Hamson. The line broke up and what she said next was garbled.

"Say that again?"

The call ended. No bars. He moved again. Two bars six feet further down the road.

"What bloody time do you call this?" asked Hamson.

"Tell me your address."

"I can't hear you."

"We need to speak, but it's best in person."

"Will it wait until tomorrow?"

"I'm already in Ham."

There was more static. Gray suspected Hamson was swearing. "I don't like bringing my work home, Sol."

"Just this once."

Hamson sighed.

"Quick, before I lose you again."

"I'm on Updown Road."

"What sort of stupid name is that?"

"Number 10 and I'll put the lights on so you can see where I am."

"Be there shortly." Gray disconnected.

Gray tapped Updown Road into the sat nav. It turned out that's where he already was, not that any signage was visible to tell him so. He started the engine, rolled the car slowly forward, drove at ten miles an hour until he hit a junction. No lights. He performed a U-turn. A few hundred yards further back from where he'd first parked a pair of bright lights shone. A drive Gray had gone straight past the first time because it was just blackness. He swung in, tyres crunching on gravel.

Hamson was standing in the doorway of a detached house, hidden from the road by trees and bushes. She was dressed in jeans and a baggy woollen jumper, arms crossed over her chest against the cold. He parked, got out. The air was still, quiet here too.

"This had better be bloody good, Sol."

"I can prove who the baby in the box is."

"That just about qualifies." She stepped out of the way. "Come in."

Hamson took Gray into the living room, turned the TV off. The curtains were wide open, nobody could see in. The furniture was mis-matched, a mix of old and new. Like she'd inherited some and bought the rest. On a nearby table sat a bottle of wine and two partly filled wine glasses.

"Got company?" he asked. Her glare was enough of an answer. As she sat down Gray said, "Amos Jenkinson."

"The pathologist? Clough's predecessor?"

"That's right," he said.

"He'd retired when I moved here so I don't really know him."

"I thought I did."

"You're sure it's him?"

"One hundred per cent. Actually 99.9."

"What?"

"Nothing."

"You've got proof?"

"A categorical yes."

"Excellent."

"And no."

"There's always a bloody 'but' with you, Sol." She picked up a glass. "Nothing for you, you're driving." She sipped. "Go on, smack me in the face with whatever you have."

"Jessop mentioned an older man in her letters."

"I haven't got dementia, tell me the new stuff."

"A witness puts Jenkinson and Jessop together in a relationship. Jessop used to dance in a club Jenkinson frequented. One of her friends there recognised his photo in the newspaper detailing his death."

"Good."

"I believe they met at Andrea Ogilvy's when Jessop was being fostered."

"Which is where the baby in the box was found, right?"

"Correct. Jenkinson was friends with the Ogilvys and used to go over regularly. And Jessop wasn't the first girl Jenkinson had a relationship with. Another woman, Kerry Hudson, confirmed they'd been together a few years before Jessop. She wouldn't reveal the man's name. She was worried about her past affecting her future. She just wanted to forget everything."

"I can hardly blame her. When you say 'girl', what age are we talking here?"

"Seventeen, Eighteen."

"Not underage, then."

"No, but vulnerable and impressionable. And Jenkinson got her pregnant."

"But she's not the mother?"

"No, it happened several years before and Hudson had a termination."

"Bloody hell."

"It appears Jenkinson targeted foster girls through his friendship with Andrea. I've no idea which came first – his friendship or the exploitation."

"Do you think Andrea was involved?"

"Hard to say. Most of the people involved in this case are dead. But I'd think probably not. Every word said about her has been positive."

"What about the daughter, Fiona?"

"She worked with Andrea. And this is where part of the puzzle still exists. Andrea was investigated because of complaints by children, what's called a Section 47. Her activities with social services were suspended. But nothing untoward was found."

"So, what's the punchline?"

"Andrea told her daughter she stopped fostering permanently because of the Section 47. But that can't have been the reason. It was lodged ten years ago, and she returned to fostering afterwards. I think the actual cause was the baby."

"God, what a mess."

"Tell me about it."

"You mentioned proof about Jenkinson."

Gray shifted in his chair. "I have a DNA profile that says the child was his. From a hair. This is where it gets more difficult."

"What's the problem?"

"I didn't get permission to take the hair sample."

"Christ." Hamson pinched the bridge of her nose. "How...?"

Gray cut her off. "Before you start into a lecture, Von, I had a thought process in mind." Hamson snorted. "I needed to categorically prove Jenkinson was the father before proceeding. All the other evidence is circumstantial, all the witnesses are either dead or very unwilling to testify. I know he for sure as hell won't."

"Let's say you're right. What's the actual reason you came out here?"

"We need a legitimate sample from Jenkinson."

"Get one from his body."

"He's being cremated tomorrow. We'd have to open his casket at the funeral directors, and we'd need permission from Fiona – the body is hers."

"Surely she'll help?"

"Not a chance. I just came from her place. She threw me out."

"Great."

"But we don't need to go down that path. She told me her father had cancer just before he died. Samples are retained at the hospital as standard procedure in case of a future need, like the disease returning. The samples will be enough to get a DNA analysis from. However, the hospital won't just hand everything over. That's why I need the warrant."

"Fiona could protest."

"Jenkinson would have signed over ownership of the samples to the hospital before they were taken. She could make a stink but if we move fast, we'll have the data before she's even aware what's gone on."

"How long?"

"The FSP got me the last analysis within the day."

Hamson thought for a few moments. "All right, I'll make some calls first thing in the morning."

"Great." Gray stood. "I have to say though, Von, your hospitality is shocking."

"You can leave now."

Thirty Two

Gray entered the QEQM mid-morning the following day, headed to Manesh's office and found the besuited Sri Lankan doctor behind his desk with a patient, the door closed. Gray waited.

Ten minutes later the patient emerged, a smile on his face. He nodded at Gray as he passed. Manesh was writing some notes when Gray entered. He looked up, his face splitting into a wide grin. He stood, a good head shorter than Gray, came from behind the desk and shook hands with gusto.

"Inspector Gray!" said Manesh. "What a pleasure to see you again!"

"Likewise, doctor."

"Is this a courtesy call?"

"Not quite. I'd appreciate your help."

"Okay." Manesh sat on the corner of the desk.

"I want to obtain a patient's tissue sample as part of an ongoing investigation." Manesh narrowed his eyes. "I have a signed warrant."

"Which I'll need to see, of course."

Gray handed his phone over, the warrant on screen already. Manesh read the document, scrolling through until he finished and passed the mobile back.

"I assume the person had cancer?" asked Manesh.

"He did. He died recently. I remember from my own treatment that tissue samples taken during that time are stored for the long term."

"We are licenced by the HTA, the Human Tissue Authority, to store and carry out research on samples taken from patients under the 2004 Human Tissue Act. They're held in the pathology department in the diagnostic archives, fixed into wax blocks or maybe microscope slides of slices. They form part of the patient's medical records and by law we have to hold them for thirty years so we can review past medical history, whether the cancer has changed over time or the potential efficacy of any new drugs that have been developed since the patient's illness occurred."

"So, you will have material?"

"We should. However, we can't always control the condition the samples are received in from the endoscopy suite or operating theatre. The fixing and storing can vary. Therefore, I can't be 100% that the samples you require are perfect."

"I'll take my chances."

"Okay." Manesh stood. "I saw the name on the warrant is Amos Jenkinson."

"That's right."

"If you can wait here, I'll have the material collected for you."

IT WAS MORE THAN AN hour before the doctor returned. Gray spent the intervening time on his phone – checking e-mail, speaking to his team about ongoing investigations and reading the news.

Manesh entered the office and closed the door. He carried a small blue chiller box by a handle. He placed it on the desk.

"I'm sorry I took so long," said Manesh. "We had some trouble locating the correct slides, particularly the older ones. The names can rub off"

"No problem." Gray pulled out his phone, dialled the courier service, waited for it to connect. "How many samples did you find?"

"Four."

"That should do."

When the motorbike courier arrived Gray handed over the box of samples and signed to confirm the transfer. As the bike whizzed out of the car park Gray sent a text to Dr Aplin. "Sample on way. Priority appreciated."

All Gray could do now was wait.

Thirty Three

Gray was checking his phone for maybe the twentieth time when Hamson entered his office.

"Still not heard?" she asked.

"The waiting is bloody killing me."

"Got time for a chat?"

"Depends whether you're going to bollock me about coming to your house last night."

"The less said about that the better. How about a coffee?"

"As long as you're buying and it's not the canteen."

"DID WE HAVE TO COME here?" asked Gray. The café was on a corner plot of the marketplace in the old town. And it sold cupcakes. Several large haphazard piles on plates sat atop the counter. Otherwise it was stripped floorboards, wooden tables and chairs, antique ephemera covering the walls.

"I like it. Besides, if you chose, we'd be in the nearest pub."

"What's wrong with The Flag?"

"Nothing, if you're a misogynist," said Hamson. Gray opened his mouth to argue, but she got in first, pointed. "There's a space come free. Go grab it."

The table was next to the floor-to-ceiling plate-glass windows which dominated the setting. Hamson joined him a few minutes later with two coffees and two cupcakes.

"I'm not eating that," said Gray. He moved the vase of flowers which sat right between them."

"Who said I got one for you?" Hamson produced a single fork and serviette. She dug into the large, fluffy cupcake topped with a white icing. "Gin and tonic flavoured."

"If they had beer flavoured, I might be slightly interested."

"You're definitely out of luck then."

Hamson finished the first cupcake.

"What's up, Von?"

"I wanted to get out for a bit. Too much time stuck at my desk."

"Good idea."

She moved onto the second cupcake. "What's happening with the dog attacks on the kids?"

"You couldn't help yourself after all."

Hamson raised her hands, fork between two fingers. "Usually I switch off when I walk through my front door."

"I'm not really making any progress."

"Do you still believe one of our colleagues is involved?"

"I'm not sure what to think. But I still don't trust Worthington."

"How is he?"

"He'll be fine. Worthington has a thick skull."

While she was prodding the remains of the cupcake with a fork she said, "What about you and Emily?"

"Why?"

"We've been talking."

Gray thought back to the two wine glasses he'd seen in Hamson's living room. "Was she at your place?"

"Yes, she made herself scarce when you rang. She thinks there's something up. She's worried, says you're even more withdrawn than usual."

"She's imagining it."

"The 'it' being Melanie Pfeffer?" Gray's mouth fell open. "I've seen how Melanie looks at you. And if I've spotted something you can bloody well bet Emily has too."

Gray's phone rang. Perfect timing.

Abbott. Not so perfect.

"I have to take this." Gray went outside.

"I've got something for you," said Abbott. "You might call it a clue."

GRAY PARKED ON ROYAL Esplanade and walked the short distance to the Sunken Gardens. He'd left Hamson in the café, not bothering to go back in. He'd never escape otherwise.

Abbott sat on a wall in the gardens. Beside him was a dog, a German Shepherd. Abbott had hold of his collar. The dog sat calmly, quietly.

"This is the clue," he said.

"A dog?"

"Not a dog, *the* dog."

"You're not making any sense."

"No wonder crime rates are so high round here. I figured it was just a question of time before whoever the geezer was after the kids would finish the job and go after Kirton. So, me and some mates shadowed the lad whenever he went out."

"Mates?"

"You know." Abbott shrugged a shoulder. "Anyway, earlier on this happened." Abbott passed over his phone. There was a video on screen. Gray pressed play. The footage was jerky and captured from a distance. It revealed somebody walking with a dog towards another person – presumably Kirton. Then the dog was on Kirton, snapping and snarling.

The footage jerked up and down as Abbott ran towards the dog owner, a shouted swear word clear over the rustling. There was a view of grass, then sky, before a brief glimpse of the dog-owner running away. Without the dog. Gray pressed stop.

"When we chased the bloke, he cleared off but Kirton got hold of the dog. The animal seemed confused when his owner cleared off" said Abbott. "Now you can find out who he is."

"How?"

"A lot of dogs have identity chips these days, in case they get lost. Which this one is." Abbott grinned. "So, he's all yours, take him."

Abbott stood, kept his finger under the collar until Gray took over. Abbott began to walk away.

"Have you got a lead?" shouted Gray.

"Use your belt," answered Abbott over his shoulder.

ACCORDING TO THE MAP app on Gray's phone the nearest vets was just off the main road in Westbrook, under a mile to the west. Gray bundled the dog into the back of his car. No tag on the collar. He drove to the vets, parked outside the church opposite, before taking the dog inside.

A woman in a blue uniform sat behind the counter directly in front of the door. She appeared vaguely like a nurse. To his left a rectangular waiting area opened up. Three equally spaced doors were inset into the longest wall and at the far end a shelf arrangement filled with cat food, dog food and toys, took up most of the space. A couple of other pet owners were already waiting. A man with a rabbit, another with a cat. Both stared at Gray.

"Can I help?" asked the receptionist. She smiled brightly.

"Do you have a chip reader here? For dogs?"

"Pardon?"

"I found him wandering around, I thought if he had a tag then I could return him."

"Oh, that's very good of you."

"Just doing my bit for the animals."

"Wait there a moment." The receptionist left her domain and disappeared behind a door.

Gray turned to face the waiting area. The man with the cat stared at the belt in Gray's hand, linked to the dog's collar.

"Sir?" A man dressed in a similar design, but dark blue, the shirt with short sleeves, stepped out of the nearest door. "Come on through."

Gray entered a small box shape room devoid of natural light. Immediately in front was a table, the surface just above Gray's hip, upon which stood a small handheld scanner. Further back was a narrow desk and computer. A couple of posters advertising dog food were stuck to one wall, in the corner a set of scales. The vet closed the door behind Gray, and the dog sat, tongue lolling. The space felt rather tight.

"Let's see what we can find, then," said the vet. "I'm Rory by the way." He grabbed the scanner, gave the dog a stroke.

"Beautiful specimen, I expect the owner will be delighted to get him back."

"Maybe."

Rory gave Gray a curious glance before he placed the scanner on the back of the dog's neck. It bleeped and a long number came up on the screen. "Here we go." The vet took the scanner over to the computer, woke up the screen. "Every chip has a unique code which is stored on a database." Rory clicked away. "Ah, yes. The owner is one of our customers and this fine beast is called Tony." Rory straightened up, turned back to Gray. "If you want you can leave him here and we'll get the owner to pick him up."

"I'd rather take Tony around myself."

The vet sucked in air through clenched teeth. "I'd like to help, but I can't give out those details. Data protection, you see."

Gray pulled out his warrant card, showed it to Rory. "Name and address, please."

Thirty Four

The house was a three-storey terrace on Upper Grove, just outside of central Margate, right next to an industrial unit, which was shuttered. The streets here were narrow and parking restricted to local residents for which privilege they had to pay –a council scam as far as Gray was concerned.

As there weren't any spaces, Gray put his car on double yellows right outside, just beyond a roller door and against the bumper of the legally parked car in front. He scribbled a note on a piece of paper which said, "Police" and left it in the window.

Leaving Tony in the car Gray headed to the nearest house. The lowest level was a basement beneath the pavement. Steps led to the middle floor. The house was well tended and neat. Gray went up the steps, knocked.

The man who opened up had damp hair, was wearing a Joy Division t-shirt, a red mark on his cheekbone and an expression of surprise on his features. "Sol, what are you doing here?"

"I've got your dog, Damian."

Boughton stared at Gray for a long moment. "You'd better bring him in then."

TONY THE DOG LAY ON the hearth rug. "He's named after Tony Wilson." Boughton shouted through from the kitchen where he was making a drink. "The guy who ran Factory Records back in the 80s and 90s."

"Okay." Gray didn't really care. He stood in the living room. Music posters adorned the walls. Four large speakers in each corner, pointing towards an armchair set in the centre of the room, which itself faced a stereo system and shelves of records, each encased in a plastic sleeve. Boughton returned, saw what Gray was staring at.

"I collect Factory stuff. It's a fascinating story, turned the industry upside down."

"I'm not really into music."

"You're missing out. Drives the wife mad, though. I'll put something on. How about a bit of Crispy Ambulance?" Boughton started to flick through the stack of records.

"Would Tony happen to be an ex-police dog?"

"That's right. He'd come to the end of his useful working life, apparently. Got plenty left in you, haven't you boy?" Tony lifted his head, then lay back down.

"Don't you want to know where I found him?" asked Gray.

Boughton slid the record out, holding it carefully at the edge. "He's back." Boughton blew on the record. "Which is all that counts." He placed the record on the turntable, started it rotating, dropped the arm. A crackle came through the speakers when the needle touched. "Not many people have heard of these guys."

Gray listened briefly, said, "I can understand why."

"Do you want something else on instead?"

"What I want you to tell me is why you've been setting your dog on kids?"

"Eh? It's Worthington."

"As much as I'd like to believe that I know it's you." Boughton knelt down, stroked Tony's head behind the ears. "The people who chased you were lying in wait. They suspected you'd go after Kirton eventually. They reeled him out as bait, and you swallowed him down."

Boughton moved over to the stereo, lifted the arm and moved further towards the centre of the record. "This song is better." He dropped the needle.

"It was Abbott who handed me your dog," said Gray. "He told me he'd landed a punch on the owner. Nice scuff you've got on your face there."

"You can't prove any of this."

"I probably could, with enough time. I'd be able to find out when you were in the station and compare it to the logon details for each of the kids attacked."

"That was Worthington, not me. The records say so."

"No, they say somebody with his credentials logged on. Kirton, Durrant and Abbott – they're all problems on your patch."

"All this is tenuous at best."

"You know me, Damian. Do you think I'll stop digging?"

The record finished. Boughton said, "I live here, Sol. I'm Margate born and bred. Most of the cops in the station are incomers. They don't know what the island used to be like, how could they? Even if I'd retired after doing my thirty years in the service those three and their mates would still be kicking around, causing trouble for everyone, including me. As I get to be an old man do you think they'd leave me alone? A pig who'd picked them up time after time? No chance. They'd make my life hell."

"You should have let the law deal with them."

"The law? Jesus, Sol, you sound like Judge Dredd." Another reference Gray didn't get. "*The law*, as you put it, totally failed me and the citizens on my beat and will continue to do so. We've had our ranks stripped to the bone, the courts are overloaded with cases, the jails are full. All in just a few short years since the credit crunch." Boughton threw his arms up, warming to his argument now. "Sure, there's talk from the politicians about reversing the trend, but how long will it take? A damn sight longer to rebuild than destroy, that's for sure. And in the meantime, who's on the front line holding back the crap, Sol? Me and you, that's who. And in between a whole generation of relatively lawless bastards are growing up with nobody to deal with them. So, I decided to."

"I understand, Damian."

"I knew you would. I tried to talk to you about all this, right at the beginning. After I realised my mistake with the Kirton kid. When we were outside the Ogilvy's."

"I don't remember."

"I said it was urgent we speak. I was going to try again, but I bottled it. I didn't think you'd be keen."

"I'd never have supported this kind of misplaced justice."

"Are you going to take me in? Make an example of me? Undermine the already low view the public has of the police?"

"I don't want to."

"That's what I thought."

"But I will if I must."

"Jesus, Sol." Boughton flopped down in his chair. "It'll be a disaster."

"You should have thought of that before setting Tony loose."

"I did. And went ahead anyway."

"Take retirement, Damian. You've done plenty of time, you'll be okay."

"Retire?"

"You said yourself you don't enjoy the job anymore."

"It's all I've got left and the pension isn't what it was once the Tories stripped it back."

"There's your wife."

"When we speak."

"And your music."

"Being stuck inside these four walls?"

"Better these than the inside of a prison cell, surely?"

"What will I do with myself?"

"Security for one of the superstores, maybe. I'm sure they'll value your experience. And it'll bring some cash in."

"Great."

"I'm handing you a lifeline here. You've got twenty-four hours to decide. Put your retirement request into Hamson by this time tomorrow or I'll be back."

Thirty Five

The call from Aplin came in much later than Gray expected. "We had some trouble," she said. "The samples you obtained hadn't been stored well so we found some degradation. Ironically it was the most recent material which proved to be poor."

"This doesn't sound good," said Gray.

"Thankfully, whoever pulled everything together included a much older sample, which had been properly preserved. And from that we were able to carry out the DNA analysis."

Gray wanted to scream, *Come on!* Instead he said, "And?"

"We found a match. The baby in the box, the hair sample you provided, and these organ materials all coincide. Your subject is the father of the child."

"I KNOW YOU'RE THERE." Gray spoke through the closed front door. He'd heard movement after he'd knocked, seen a twitch at the window. Fiona was in, for sure.

"What do you want?" She was on the other side of the wood, listening.

"To talk."

"Go away."

"I can't do that."

"Leave me alone."

"Fiona, we're going to speak whether you like it or not. Either open up or I'll say what I have to in the middle of the street."

"No."

"I have solid proof."

"I don't believe you."

"I have a DNA profile that matches. From the hospital. From your father's cancerous cells."

"So?"

"Just think of the scandal it would cause." Gray listened for a moment, heard nothing. "Okay, have it your way."

Gray headed to the adjacent house and rang the bell.

The homeowner, an elderly woman, opened up. "Hello young man."

"Stop!" Fiona, running over. "Stop!"

"What on earth is going on?" asked the old woman. Fiona began to drag Gray away.

"I'm sorry for disturbing you," said Gray.

The old woman watched Fiona and Gray until Fiona had Gray inside and the door closed.

Breathing heavily Fiona said, "Why are you doing this to me?"

"You lied."

"I need a drink." She headed down the corridor towards the rear of the house. Gray followed. She entered a conservatory, which overlooked the garden. Gray had been in here before, talking to Jenkinson about an old case, before the Alzheimer's had really taken hold. Fiona poured herself a large measure of brandy, took a gulp, then another, wiped her mouth. She topped up the glass, waved the bottle at Gray. "I suppose you won't want one, being on duty?"

"All I'm after are answers."

"Good God, Sol. You should hear yourself."

"Your father got Zara Jessop pregnant."

"He didn't."

"I told you, I have categorical proof. I have a match this morning. He's the father of the baby in the box. It's undeniable"

"Where did you get a sample?"

"The hospital, they keep them in cold storage."

"You're not allowed to take them. They don't belong to you."

"And you knew all about what your father had done."

"Not true." The lie didn't sound convincing.

"It was you who took the baby over to Andrea. Asked Andrea to look after her."

"No."

"You were friends with Andrea, you were there regularly."

"Stop it." Fiona had another drink.

"You couldn't stand the idea of a scandal, that your father, a respected member of the community, had got a young woman pregnant. A whore, as you put it."

"It would have killed my mother."

"It killed Zara. She died alone, in her flat, drunk."

"I couldn't help that."

Gray couldn't speak for a few moments, shocked at how callous Fiona sounded. Fiona's shoulders began to shake.

Fiona wiped the back of her hand across her nose. There were tears in her eyes. "All these years I thought the baby was alive, growing up. Because Andrea told me she'd found a home for her." Fiona paused. "So, when you told me about the corpse, I couldn't believe it. She'd lied to me."

"We believe the girl died of natural causes, probably very soon after you took her over."

"And Andrea just hid her?"

"So, it seems. She probably thought there was nothing else she could do. Who could she turn to? There wasn't even a record of the birth."

"Oh my God."

"It was all a tragic accident."

"She must have felt trapped for years," said Fiona. "We both did. Thank you for telling me." She smiled, relieved.

"This isn't the end."

"What do you mean?"

"It wasn't just you who was friends with Andrea. So was your father. That's how he got to know Zara." Gray paused. "And the others."

"Others?"

"Kerry Hudson. He got her pregnant too."

"What?"

"But she had the pregnancy terminated and stayed quiet because she was scared of what your father might do to her."

"No, this can't be true."

"I strongly suspect there will be more, if I keep going."

"Why would you do this to me, Sol? Why?"

"I know your father undermined your relationship with Ben Clough."

Fiona raised the glass, spun and threw it at a large framed photo of her father and mother together. The glass shattered, shredding the image, splattering it with liquid. Fiona turned away from Gray, her shoulders heaving as she breathed deeply. Slowly, she faced Gray again.

"He destroyed everything for me."

"Why did you keep quiet?"

"For my mother, I loved her. Then she died. I walked away, but he got dementia."

"What happened in the flat with Zara? When you took the baby from her."

Fiona sagged down into a chair, all the fight gone out of her. Gray sat opposite, waited. Eventually she said, "Zara was a mess, she couldn't cope. She didn't have family locally and the baby was driving her to her wits end. She was struggling for money too. So, I offered to take the pressure off her and remove the baby." Fiona fixed Gray's eyes. "She was happy I did that, Sol. You need to believe me."

"I do."

"That's when I took the baby to Andrea's. It was late at night, nobody was around. No paperwork, either. It was only supposed to be for a couple of days. I told Andrea if she knew anybody who wanted a baby then they could have this one. I left.

"Then Zara kept calling me, saying she wanted her baby back, that it had all been a big mistake. I went over to Andrea's. But she told me the baby had gone, that a couple had taken her."

"And you believed her?"

"Of course. I thought Andrea was as straight as they came. I asked who the couple were, but Andrea wouldn't tell me. Said they were from out of town and it was best I didn't know their names."

"It's tenuous."

"I'm aware how it sounds now, but back then I was highly stressed. I just needed a solution, any solution. I went over to Zara's. She was drunk already. There was no way she could have had the baby back in that state and I told her. She came at me with a bottle, but she tripped and banged her head. She collapsed. I tried to wake her up, but she was dead, Sol. I panicked, came straight here, to this house and told Dad. He said he'd fix everything. He made a few calls – to your old friend, Jeff Carslake."

"Good God."

"And everything did get fixed. The death was ruled accidental and before long Zara was forgotten about by everybody except me, Andrea, and Dad. That's why I came back and looked after him. Because he knew what happened and he wouldn't let me forget it. If I'd been aware of everything else, I'd have taken my chances and left him to rot." A silence fell between them for a while until Fiona said, "So, are you going to take me in, as they say?"

"I have to."

"I know." Fiona stood. "There's one more thing to tell you. The baby had a name. Sophia."

Thirty Six

The obvious place to meet was Andrea's old house on Ranelagh Grove. It was almost empty now, just the largest pieces of furniture like the sofas, sideboards and table. The pictures were all packed and gone.

The three of them were seated in the living room: Ogilvy, Draper and Gray. He was facing the curtainless window.

"Thanks for agreeing to see me," said Gray.

"I haven't got long," said Ogilvy, dour as ever.

"Shut up then, Philip," said Draper. Ogilvy glared at her. "Go on, Inspector."

"This will all be in the papers soon. They've already got wind of Fiona's arrest."

"I couldn't believe it when I heard," said Draper.

"What happened to shutting up?" said Ogilvy. Draper rolled her eyes. He asked, "And what's our connection to all of this?"

"Your mother was entirely blameless. Jenkinson used their friendship and her vulnerable charges to look for potential partners."

"Grooming?" asked Draper.

"Kind of. Fiona learned her father had got one girl, Zara Jessop, pregnant. She didn't want the scandal, so she used her position too for her own benefit. She brought the baby here. We now know the baby was called Sophia.

"Not long after Sophia's arrival here it seemed she passed away. We're assuming your mother hid the body because she was worried about what might happen to her. Understandable after the previous troubles she'd faced."

"And Zara died?"

"That's right. For now, I can't say any more about that subject."

Draper and Ogilvy shared a glance.

"Our father must be turning in his grave with shame," said Ogilvy.

"Don't be ridiculous, Philip," snapped Draper. "He loved Mum and would have supported her regardless."

"I know, but all this, it's..."

"What? What is it?"

"Distasteful."

Draper stood, loomed over her brother. "She always came second to everyone else's needs. And you sit there, judging her. Do you know what our mother did for you? What she gave up?"

"Me? What have I got to do with all this?"

"You're as much part of the problem as anyone else. Making Mum put aside her feelings."

"You're making no sense. You're as crazy as she is. I can't believe we're related."

"We're not, Philip!"

"What the hell are you on about?" Draper realised what she'd said, put a hand over her mouth. "Tell me."

"We have different fathers. Mum was pregnant with you when they got married."

"Dad isn't related to me?"

"No."

"Why are you only telling me this now, and in front of him?" Ogilvy pointed at Gray.

"I wasn't ever going to tell you, and he knows. From the DNA testing."

"Jesus." Ogilvy rounded on Gray. "Why did you not come to me?"

"It's nothing to do with Inspector Gray," said Draper. She flopped down into her seat. "Mum let it out years ago. Inspector Gray didn't raise our relationship. That was me."

"I don't believe this." Ogilvy put his head into his hands.

"I'm sorry. I didn't mean for everything to come out like this. I never intended it to come out at all."

Ogilvy slowly raised his eyes onto Draper. "No, you're not sorry. This is so much like you." He stood. "Once the sale on this place goes through there's no reason for us to see each other again."

"Philip." Ogilvy walked out. "Philip!" The front door slammed. Draper let out a lungful of air. "I apologise for you having to witness that."

Gray raised a palm. "No problem."

"Actually, I'm glad it's all out in the open. I'm sick of keeping secrets. There have been too many of them over the years."

"Do you believe him? That you won't see each other again?"

"It's Philip, you never quite know what you're getting. It's important for him to be aware of his past. We should all know where we come from."

"Maybe."

"Anyway," Draper stood. "It's done now. There's no taking that back."

Outside, Gray recalled what Draper had said; about knowing your past. He pulled out his phone and called Dr Aplin at the DNA labs.

Thirty Seven

Gray knocked on the door.

"Inspector," said Kerry Hudson when she opened up. "I wasn't expecting you."

"I won't be long."

"Come in."

This time Gray got beyond the hall, into the living room.

"I read about everything in the papers. Such a shame. Do you think she'll be sent to prison?"

"That's not up to me now. And I'm here to talk about you, not Fiona Jenkinson. Or more precisely, your mother."

"My mother?"

"As a favour I asked the lab who originally assessed your DNA to see if they could find a match to anyone in the database." Gray held out an envelope. "Her name is in there."

But Hudson didn't take it. "Why?"

"You told me you didn't know who your parents were. This gives you part of an answer, if you want it." Hudson placed a hand across her open mouth, eyes wide. "Sorry, I wasn't sure how else to tell you." Gray put the envelope down on a nearby table. "Burn it if you want."

Gray was on the pavement nearing his car when Hudson called. "Inspector Gray, wait!" She ran towards him, clutching the envelope. She threw her arms out, enveloped him in a big hug. "Thank you! I can't tell you how much it means to know something, at last."

When Gray had extricated himself he said, "It was the least I could do."

"You didn't have to, and I appreciate that. I apologise for my reaction; I just wasn't expecting that."

"I'd better go."

"Criminals to catch?"

"Something like that. Good luck with the wedding."

Thirty Eight

The gathering was small, just a handful of people attending the committal ceremony. It proved brief. The few words read by the vicar echoed around the cavernous interior of St. Peter's church. A couple of hymns were sung, the organ drowning out the accompanying voices. No eulogies by relatives because, how could you?

It was raining when they moved outside – the tiny coffin in front being carried by Zara's brother, Edgar along the narrow tarmac path, then the vicar, Draper and, finally, Gray.

Neither Zara's parents nor Philip Ogilvy attended. Gray could just about accept his absence; after all, what was his connection to the child? But Zara's relatives were a different matter. They were blood and their grandchild was being buried.

The vicar stopped beside the plot. The earth had been dug back, producing a deep hole. The small coffin was lowered into it. The vicar read a prayer. And then they were done. The vicar shook hands with Edgar, then Draper and Gray before he walked back to the church. Gray stood, not sure what to do next.

There was a stone to be erected too. With the baby's name, Sophia Jessop, carved on it.

"Thanks for coming," said Edgar to both of them.

"It's the least I can do," said Draper.

"Likewise," said Gray.

"Where are your parents?"

"They're otherwise engaged." Edgar pursed his lips, like he'd sucked on a lemon. "My mother and I had long overdue words. My father took her side so I'm persona non grata right now."

"At least you're here for your sister."

"Somebody should be."

"I really appreciate what you did, Inspector," said Edgar. "Giving up your plot for Sophia. Sophia was our grandmother's name. She doted on Zara. Grandma Sophia and my mother didn't get along." Edgar smiled. "Which would be another reason for Zara's choice of name."

"It's Sol, and no problem. The space was going to waste otherwise. Just somewhere for weeds to grow." Gray's wife had bought space for herself and their son. But Tom didn't need it.

"Nevertheless. Zara, next to her daughter, Sophia. And Zara near to your wife all along." Edgar held his hand out for Gray to shake.

Movement caught Gray's eye. He glanced up. Across the graveyard, behind Edgar's shoulder, stood a man leaning on a stick, staring at Gray. Despite being partially masked by the trees, Gray recognised him immediately.

"Is everything all right?" asked Draper.

"Fine," lied Gray. "There's just somebody I need to speak with."

Draper said, "If you've got time to spare, we can have a drink at my house."

"I'd like that."

"See you there."

Draper and Edgar turned to walk away.

Gray headed across to Frank McGavin. Living abroad seemed to have been good for him. He'd developed a deep tan. McGavin was a big man, broad and tall, dominating every space he inhabited.

"Perfect place for you, this," said Gray. "Among the gravestones."

"I like the dead, Sol. They keep their secrets." McGavin grinned. Teeth glowed bright, like they'd been whitened artificially. "Have you missed me?"

"As much as I miss a kick in the bollocks."

McGavin chuckled. "So that's a yes, then."

"What do you want?"

"I've already got the best gift you could give me." McGavin pointed at him.

"I can't be doing with your bullshit games." Gray turned away.

"Jerry Worthington."

Gray stopped, pivoted back to face McGavin. "Pardon?"

"I know what you did." Gray waited. "Not taking the bait? I'll give you a name. Andrew Abbott."

"Never heard of him."

"He knows you, though. Says you told him who set a dog on his son." McGavin paused again, stared intently at Gray.

Gray stepped forward, got into McGavin's personal space. "You can't prove anything. My words against yours. Cop against crook."

"Really, Inspector?" The derision was clear in McGavin's tone. He pushed Gray, made him take a step back again. McGavin spoke quietly. "You're mine now. Do you understand?"

Gray didn't answer.

After a moment McGavin straightened, patted Gray on the shoulder. "I'll give you some time to get used to the idea. I'll be in touch at some point."

Thirty Nine

Gray left his car and walked to Draper's. It was only a few minutes' stroll. He rapped on the glass, McGavin's final words still on his mind.

Draper opened up. Gray expected the dog to be at his ankles, wagging his tail, but he wasn't.

"Where's Mack?" Gray asked as he stepped inside. "Are you keeping him out of the way?"

Draper's expression drooped. "My husband finally put his foot down. We couldn't keep him, so he's gone."

"Where?"

"The rescue centre over in Flete. I drove him yesterday. Broke my heart, but we had to." Draper closed the door. "The woman that runs the place, I can't remember her name, says they'll find a home for him. It might take some time, though."

"Why?"

"Terriers aren't popular because they're a handful. If Mack was a labradoodle or some other combination of breeds, he'd be out of there in seconds, but for a variety like Mack it might run to months."

"Months?"

"Easily, maybe even more."

"Oh."

"At least it's not one of those places that put animals down if no one has taken them after a certain amount of time."

Gray had read about the kennels where there were too many dogs to be housed so the excess had to be selectively euthanised. He'd never really considered the inhumanity of the situation until now.

"Do you mind if I don't stay?"

Draper blinked, caught off guard. "Sure."

"I've got someone to see about a dog."

Draper grinned; the confusion gone. "Under the circumstances, no problem at all."

"THAT'S HIM." GRAY STOOD beside a pen. Mack's front paws were up on the barrier, his tail wagging, tongue out.

"Well, there are two options," said Amy, the manager of the animal shelter. The place was located down a dirt track, right on the edge of Margate, in the flat, empty land between Manston airport and the Westwood Cross shopping centre. "Fostering or adoption. With fostering you look after the dog at home, but he remains the property of the shelter. With adoption you take him on as your own."

"I think fostering is out."

"Have you owned a dog before?"

"A few years ago now." Like about thirty-five, when Gray was a kid and the responsibility was strictly someone else's.

"That's good."

"Can I take him now?"

"Usually we carry out a home visit, to check you and the location are suitable."

"Oh, okay."

"But as you're a police officer and we usually have difficult rehoming terriers I'm sure we can come to an arrangement."

"That's great, thanks."

"All I need are some personal details and a donation towards his upkeep."

"Sure." Gray didn't point out Mack had been with them less than a day. The shelter was a charity, after all.

"If you'll follow me, we'll get started."

Gray left Mack and sorted out all the paperwork with Amy. Just over a quarter of an hour later he was back, lead in Amy's hand. He'd bought all the essentials too, like a bowl, a basket and some food. They were in the back of the car.

She went inside, clipped the lead onto Mack's collar, came out and handed it to Gray. "I hope you'll be happy together."

"Come on, boy," said Gray. "Let's go home."

THE END

Other Novels by Keith Nixon

The Solomon Gray Series
Dig Two Graves
Burn The Evidence
Beg For Mercy
Bury The Bodies
Pity The Dead
The Silent Dead
Betray Them All
The Dead Can't Lie
The Jonah Pennance Series
Blood Sentence
Dead Money
The Konstantin Series
Russian Roulette
My Middle Name Is Misery
Dark Heart, Heavy Soul
I'm Dead Again
The Fix
The Harry Vaughan Series
The Nudge Man
The DI Granger Series
The Corpse Role
The Caradoc Series
The Eagle's Shadow

The Eagle's Blood

244

About The Author

Keith Nixon is a British born writer of crime and historical fiction novels. Originally, he trained as a chemist, but Keith is now in a senior sales role for a high-tech business.

Keith currently lives with his family in the North-West.

Page of 131

www.ingramcontent.com/pod-product-compliance
Lightning Source LLC
Chambersburg PA
CBHW072009170726
47999CB00014B/1365